flowers _____ ve
Henry _____ ns.
Wildly _____ JUN 2 2 1996 __ searching for the plant that
Henry had described.

Ethan dropped to his knees. Tears ran down his face as
he searched frantically among the weeds and wildflowers. If
only he knew what he was looking for!

"You look for something?"

Startled, Ethan whipped around to find a tall sun-
browned man behind him. An Indian! How could he have
come out of nowhere so silently? Ethan crouched in the
grass and stared at the man in terror. Black hair hung in
one braid down the Indian's back. He wore soft buckskin
leggings and jacket. A large bow hung over his shoulder,
but he also carried a rifle on one arm. Was he friendly?

PRAIRIE HOMESTEAD

by Arleta Richardson

Chariot Books™
A Division of Cook Communications

Chariot Books™ is an imprint of David C. Cook Publishing Co.
David C. Cook Publishing Co., Elgin, Illinois 60120
David C. Cook Publishing Co., Weston, Ontario
Nova Distribution Ltd., Eastbourne, England

PRAIRIE HOMESTEAD
© 1994 by Arleta Richardson

Cover design by Helen Lannis, interior design by Mark Novelli
Cover illustration by Patrick Soper
First Printing, 1994
Printed in the United States of America

98 97 96 95 94   5 4 3 2 1

Library of Congress Cataloging-in-Publication Data
Richardson, Arleta.
Prairie homestead / Arleta Richardson.
p.   cm.—(The orphans' journey; 3)
Summary: Eight-year-old orphan Ethan and his three younger siblings are taken in by the
Rush family and find themselves homesteading in South Dakota.
ISBN 0-7814-0091-0
[1. Orphans—Fiction. 2. Frontier and pioneer life—Fiction. 3. South Dakota—Fiction. 4.
Christian life—Fiction.] I. Title. II. Series: Richardson, Arleta. Orphans' journey ; bk. 3.
PZ7.R3942Pr   1994
[Fic]—dc20   94-27086
                                                                            CIP
                                                                            AC

Contents

With warm regards to
Bud and Jane Fisher
and in memory of
Margaret

Introduction

Nine-year-old Ethan Cooper, his sister Alice, and brothers Simon and Will were sent west on the Orphan Train with the hope that life for them would be better than the one they could have in a county children's home.

Homeless children like the Coopers were "farmed out" with the best of intentions of the authorities. They were expected to adjust to the ways of Midwestern farm homes. These ways included hard work, strict and sometimes harsh discipline, and, in some cases, a minimum of love and attention. The fact that the majority of these children grew to be respectable, hardworking adults speaks well for the strength of the human spirit.

The Cooper children were adopted by Chad and Manda Rush, a prosperous couple with one adopted daughter already in their home. Because of their own upbringing, the Rushes had difficulty expressing affection to each other or to their children. The coming of the four young Coopers caused them to reevaluate their relationship to God and to their family.

In the spring of 1909, the Rushes moved their household to a prairie homestead in South Dakota. Life on the plains was not easy. Unpredictable weather and the difficulty of cultivating the wilderness land took its toll on all of them. The excitement of living in a soddy grew thin. But the man whose life was the basis of Ethan's story later said, "It was there that I learned to trust God completely, to develop a respect for the land, and to know the love of a family. It was a hard road, but it taught me much about life."

Learning to rely on God in every circumstance was a value that "Ethan" handed down to his children. Surely there is no greater heritage he could have bestowed upon them.

Arleta Richardson
1994

GOING HOME

The huge engine chugged and puffed, and a short whistle announced that the train was ready to leave. The little town of Willow Creek, Nebraska, was not a regular stop for the afternoon passenger coach. But today was a special occasion, and it seemed that most of the town and the surrounding communities were on hand to observe it. The Orphan Train from Chicago had brought five children to be adopted, and all the townspeople wanted to see them, whether they planned to take a child or not.

Ethan Cooper, holding tightly to his two younger brothers, looked back at the train that had been the children's home for two weeks. There was a hollow feeling in Ethan's stomach as he thought of all that was familiar disappearing in a cloud of steam. Of course he did have Simon and Will and his little sister, Alice.

Alice tugged at his jacket. "Are we going with that man, Ethan?"

"When Mr. Glover tells us to, we will," Ethan replied. "We want to be sure the right people take us."

The crowd milling about was confusing. There were a lot more grown-ups here than there were children to be placed in homes. In fact, only two couples would take home orphans today, for the four Cooper children were promised to one family. The only other boy who had come this far was Ethan's best friend, Bert.

Cheerful, freckle-faced Bert had been Ethan's ally since the Coopers had arrived at Briarlane Christian Children's Home a year ago. When it was decided that both boys would ride the Orphan Train west, they were delighted to be able to stay together a little longer. But Bert was skeptical of the program when they stopped at the first small town.

"They're going at this backwards. Us kids need to pick the ma and pa we'd like, 'stead of them picking us. The ones I want ain't out there. My ma had curly soft hair around her face. Theirs is all pulled back tight. And my pa would be dancing a jig to make folks laugh. I don't see 'em."

As it turned out, Bert was given a choice among the families who waited at the station. He chose Carl and Hannah Boncoeur, a young couple homesteading north of Willow Creek. Now Ethan turned to watch Bert walk away with his new parents. Hannah still had her arm around his shoulder, and Carl walked with a bounce in his step that made Ethan smile, in spite of the heaviness in his heart. Bert had wanted a father who "would dance a jig on the

station platform," and Carl's obvious delight in getting the
boy assured Bert that he had found what he wanted. Ethan
was happy for him.

"Well, are you ready?"

The cold voice of Chad Rush brought Ethan back to his
own situation.

"Yes, sir. I'd like to say good-bye to Mr. Glover and
Matron."

"Be quick about it."

All of them solemnly shook hands with Agent Glover,
then they were warmly hugged by Matron Daly.

"Be good children," she admonished them. "Write to us
and let us know how you are getting on in your new home.
Remember, the Lord will be with you. He promised never
to leave you or forsake you. You know you can pray to Him
anytime."

Ethan nodded and clutched the big key in his pocket.
Bert had given it to him as a token of their friendship.

"Pa gave it to me," Bert had said. "He said it's the key to
success, because whenever you feel it, it reminds you to
pray—and that's the way to be successful."

Already Ethan was grateful for the solid reminder. He
didn't feel as sure of their welcome as he would have liked,
but he couldn't let the little ones know. They depended on
him. Ethan turned once more toward the train, and
watched as the conductor picked up the step in front of the
door and climbed back into the car.

The children followed Chad and Manda Rush to the
buggy. Ethan lifted Will in, then helped Simon and Alice

to climb up to the seat.

"Ethan, are we going to our own home now?" Simon looked anxiously at his older brother.

Ethan smiled at him. "Yes, Simon. We're going to our own home now."

"Do they want us?" Simon's big eyes mirrored his concern.

"Of course they do. They wouldn't have asked for us if they didn't want us."

Simon appeared satisfied and settled down to watch the landscape as they headed out into the country.

Maybe the Rushes didn't know what they were getting, Ethan thought. He wondered especially about the older, solemn-looking girl who sat facing them in the buggy. This must be the big sister, Frances, they had been told to expect. She had not said a word to any of them, not even to Alice, who watched her carefully.

The ride seemed like a long one to Ethan, since no one spoke. Mile after mile of open country went by with nothing to be seen but newly plowed land, some cattle, and an occasional fence. Whom did it all belong to?

"Papa owns all this land," Frances said suddenly, as though she had heard what he was thinking. "He owns it all on the other side of the house too."

There seemed to be nothing to say in reply to this bit of news, so Ethan just nodded.

"Where is the house?" Alice whispered in his ear.

"I don't know, but I'm sure we'll see it pretty soon," Ethan replied softly.

"I don't think they like us very much."

"It's not proper to whisper," Frances said primly. "People will think you're talking about them."

"Alice wonders where the house is," Ethan replied. "We haven't seen any barns or anything."

"It's up there past the trees. We're almost home now."

Alice looked at Frances with wide eyes, and Ethan stared ahead at the stiff backs of Chad and Manda. Why hadn't their new parents welcomed them or asked any questions? He and the others might have been four bags of feed they had come to pick up in town. Ethan grinned at the thought.

"What are you laughing at?" Frances demanded.

Ethan straightened his face and mumbled, "Nothing."

"Well, you look awfully silly setting there grinning to yourself."

Ethan looked away and sighed. This was a long trip home.

The sun was beginning to set when Luke and Henry, Chad Rush's hired hands, threw down the last forkful of hay and closed the barn door for the night.

Henry removed his hat and mopped his face with a handkerchief. "Wonder what time they'll get back?"

"Any time now, I'd reckon. Chad won't waste the day chatting with the townsfolk. And the mood Manda was in when they left, she won't be any too friendly either." Luke chuckled as they approached the house.

"Looks like we'll have to cut a wide swath around Polly,

too. I can hear those pots bangin' clear out here."

"Can't say as I blame her," Henry replied. "The biggest
load for the care of four more children will land on her.
Don't see why Chad thought he needed 'em."

"Frances," Luke spoke briskly. "She kept after her pa for
weeks about getting another boy to replace Robbie. Chad
finally gave in to her."

As they washed up for supper, Luke thought back over
the years he had worked for Chad Rush. They had attended
school together, back in the little town of Willow Creek.
Even then, Chad had not been well-liked. He kept to
himself and had little to say to his schoolmates. But, Luke
recalled, there was no question that Chad Rush was a
winner. At everything he tried, he succeeded. From his
studies to the games they played, Chad could not be bested.
Yet he seemed to take no pride in these accomplishments,
Luke remembered. Rather, the boy's set jaw announced to
the world that nothing was going to get him down.

The whole community knew that the older Mr. Rush
had certainly tried. Frequently Chad appeared at school
with welts and dark bruises on various parts of his body.

"What happened to you, Chad? Fall out of the hay
mow?"

"My pa strapped me."

"Why? What'd you do?"

"Nothing. He didn't like the way I did my work."

Shortly after their school years ended, Chad married
Manda Scott. The elder Mr. Rush gave his son a portion of
land and his blessing. Since that time, Chad's material

wealth had increased. In the years that Luke had been overseer on the farm, there had been ample opportunity to observe Chad and Manda's style of life firsthand. Luke had been less than impressed.

Henry, however, tried occasionally to defend their employer when things were rough.

"Chad's a fair man. He does what he sees as his Christian duty. There's no one more faithful to church than he is."

"Religious he is," Luke replied, "but we don't see eye-to-eye on the 'Christian.' I think being a Christian ought to improve your disposition. It hasn't done a whole lot for them two."

Five years ago there had seemed to be hope for the Rush household. Manda had decided to adopt two children from an orphanage in the East. Reluctantly, Chad went along with the plan, and eight-year-old Frances and Robbie, almost two, had joined the family. From the first Frances had clung to Chad, while Robbie was Manda's baby.

There had been no agreement on discipline, Luke reflected, and Frances was alternately punished and pampered. When an accident to her little brother resulted in his death from pneumonia, Chad reacted by spending more time away from the house, and Manda's small store of patience became nonexistent.

"Maybe we can eat and get back to the bunkhouse before they get home."

Henry's voice brought Luke back to the present, and he wiped his hands and face on the rough towel hanging

beside the wash basin. They entered the kitchen to be met
by a stormy-faced Polly.

" 'Bout time you was getting in here. I spend all
afternoon getting supper for folks who never let me know
when they'll be home." She slammed plates down in front
of the silent men.

"Shouldn't be taking it out on you," she admitted
grudgingly. " 'Tain't your fault that Chad's got no control
over his family. He didn't have to give in to Frances."

Polly slumped into a chair at the end of the table and
stared morosely at the platter of roast beef and browned
potatoes in front of them. Big bowls of spring vegetables,
thick slices of crusty bread, and dishes of pickles, jam, and
creamy cottage cheese reflected the late afternoon sun
streaming through the window.

Luke piled his plate high before he spoke. "Won't be
easy, having four young children on the place. They'll grow
up to help some, but they'll be a lot of care."

"Frances is all the care we need," Polly retorted. "All's
the others will do is make more work."

"Manda's still mourning for Robbie," Henry offered.
"Mebbe this new young 'un will soften her heart."

"You been in the sun too long," Polly told him. "There
ain't no way to soften what ain't there." She sighed heavily.
"I think I'm just as worried about how Chad will treat those
boys," she admitted. "He won't cut 'em no slack when they
don't step to when he speaks. He'll handle a switch the
same way his pa did, I've no doubt."

The men nodded.

"If these orphans came off the streets, they'll be used to a hard life. If they've spent their lives in an orphanage, they'll probably wish they were back there." Luke transferred a piece of pie to his plate. "I wouldn't have recommended taking in four waifs, but no one asked me."

The remainder of the meal was eaten in silence, and when the men rose to go to the bunkhouse, Polly began to clear the table. A glance out the open door showed her that darkness would soon be upon them. She sighed again as she shuffled toward the dining room with plates and silverware.

"Four more people to feed from now on," she muttered. She was glad that Chad Rush kept a good table. Cooking was the only thing Polly enjoyed about her job. They had the best of meat, vegetables, and fruit, and no one interfered with her meals. However, she thought rebelliously, she hadn't signed on to feed an entire orphanage. If her ma didn't need the money she earned, Polly would leave this place in a minute.

Polly West had also attended school with Chad Rush and Manda Scott. She had been the victim of Manda's sharp tongue and ignored by Chad, as had most of her other classmates. Occasionally Polly remembered when her daydreams had placed her in Chad's favor, but years and circumstances had erased that fancy.

"Why do you stay with that disagreeable woman?" Polly's friends inquired.

"No one else to care for Ma," she replied. "I keep hoping Manda will find something to make her happy. Robbie might have done it if he'd lived."

But he didn't, she reflected as she set the table. And this group coming in wasn't likely to do it, either.

The sound of wheels in the lane announced the return of the family, and Polly hurried to take up the food. Time enough later to sort things out when she'd seen the children.

MANDA

No one really knows how news travels in a rural area. Although the buggy carrying the Cooper children, a silent Frances, and stiff-backed Chad and Manda met no other conveyance on the trip home, nor did they observe anyone in the fields as they passed by, everyone in the countryside knew that the Rushes had arrived home at dusk with not one, but four orphan children from the train.

"Never thought I'd be surprised at anything Manda Rush did," Lydia Archer said to her husband, Ben, "but I can scarce believe this. Why do you suppose they decided to take four more young ones to raise?"

"Don't expect 'they' did," Ben grunted. "Chad's outnumbered three to one by womenfolk in that house. They're the ones as'll do the raising."

"I'll wait until morning to call on her," Lydia decided, "but I mean to ask Manda for her reasons. They certainly don't need farm workers, and besides, little ones like that won't be much good."

Ben Archer shrugged his shoulders and held his tongue. He would say nothing about what Chad had hinted to him, since his plans were not common knowledge. As far as Ben knew, Chad had not yet revealed his purpose to Manda.

Ben reckoned that word would be out soon enough. Manda's reaction to the news was predictable, and Ben was glad that he would not have to be an eyewitness to it.

The buggy turned into the lane, and the Cooper children had their first glimpse of their new home. Silently they looked at the large two-story house surrounded by trees. A wide porch wrapped around three sides, and a setting sun as red as fire was reflected in the big windows.

Inside, the table was laden with more food than Ethan and the others could take in as they were hurried through the dining room to the kitchen.

"Are we going to eat out here?" Simon asked, and Ethan tried to hush him.

"Mercy, no," Polly answered. "You just need to wash up after that trip. Here—let me help."

She wet the end of a towel in the wash basin and began working on Will's face and hands. The others gathered around and wiped the grime off, careful not to splash water on the shiny linoleum floor. Polly then brushed hair and straightened clothes, and pronounced each child ready to return to the dining room. Chad was seated at one end of the table, with Frances beside him. At the other end sat

Manda. She spoke for the first time as she directed them to their seats.

"Now. Tell me your names."

"I'm Ethan, ma'am, and . . ."

Manda interrupted him. "They are all old enough to answer for themselves."

One by one the Coopers announced their names, with Will adding, "I'm three. Are you my mama and papa?"

Chad ignored the question and bowed his head to ask the blessing.

When their plates were filled, Manda spoke again.

"You may have all you want to eat. No one has ever gone hungry in this house. Anyone who is six years or older will have work to do. We will not have a lazy child on the place." She looked at Ethan. "Tomorrow morning you and Alice will be assigned your chores."

"Yes, ma'am."

This seemed to be all that Manda had to say, and the meal proceeded in silence. Polly, serving and clearing the table, did not miss anything that went on, nor did she fail to repeat it to Luke and Henry the following morning.

It was with great difficulty that she restrained her excitement until the men were served their breakfast.

"You should have stayed in the house and waited till they got back," she said. "You missed the biggest news we've had around here for a while."

"They decided not to take the children," Henry guessed.

Polly shook her head. "You're not even close. They brought 'em all home, just like they planned. Seem like nice young 'uns, but they never had a chance to speak. Manda took things in hand right away, like always. But she didn't hold the reins for very long."

The men looked at Polly expectantly.

"Just as I was bringing in the pie, Chad spoke up. 'Might as well tell you all now,' he says, 'come early spring we'll be moving to South Dakota.' "

Luke stopped with a forkful of potatoes halfway to his mouth. "Chad? Move?"

Polly nodded. "Yep. Says he has a new claim on the edge of an Indian reservation. He'll have to work it for a year and build a house. And that ain't the end of it. He's countin' on all of us going with him!"

Luke and Henry looked at each other in disbelief. Finally Henry spoke.

"What did Manda say about that?"

Polly grinned. "Not a word. She was struck witless. I'll wager she said plenty when she got him alone, but I didn't hear none of it. She just sent Frances to her room and told me to take the children to bed." Polly jumped to her feet. "Mercy! It's almost daylight. I've got to get breakfast for the family. Anyway, that'll give you something to chew on while you work this morning."

Manda paced the floor of the big living room, stopping occasionally to straighten an antimacassar on the back of a chair or move a picture an inch to the left or right. She had only picked at her breakfast, a fact not overlooked by Polly. Again there had been no conversation around the table, and when Chad left the house, he took Ethan with him. Alice was turned over to Polly, and the younger boys were sent out to explore the farm on their own. So distraught was Manda that she didn't even warn Simon to keep an eye on Will.

Homestead in South Dakota! All the previous land acquired by Chad had adjoined what he already owned and made no change in Manda's routine. But this new claim would do away with life as she knew it, and Manda was having trouble grasping the magnitude of it.

She was suddenly overcome with exhaustion and dropped into the nearest chair. Closing her eyes did nothing to dispel the picture of what lay before her. She knew there was not a possibility of changing Chad's mind, for she had tried. Polly had not been mistaken in her guess that Manda had "said plenty when she got him alone."

"Chad, whatever do you mean that we're moving to South Dakota? You know we can't do that! What will we do with all the children? What about school, and music lessons for Frances?"

"Frances will finish eighth grade this year," Chad replied calmly. "I reckon she can teach the others while we're there. We have to live on the land, or I'll lose it."

"But a house!" Manda wailed. "What are we going to live in?"

"Henry and I will go up and get a place ready. We can dig a soddy in a couple of weeks."

Manda's mouth opened, but no sound came out. Five children and five adults in a soddy! There was no possible way she could live like that.

"We'll build a bunkhouse for the men," Chad went on. "Ethan can stay in with them. You'll have all winter to do your packing."

Chad seemed to think that he had taken care of all the problems, Manda reflected. He had no idea what it took to run a household. Food, clothing, laundry, and cleaning weren't his responsibilities. Besides, they hadn't even begun to get acquainted with these new children. How could Chad do such a thing? Manda's head pounded so hard that it was several moments before she realized that someone was knocking on the door. She opened it to Lydia Archer.

"Manda! You look awful! Did those children keep you up all night? Where are they?"

"Good morning, Lydia. Come in and sit down."

Manda led the way into the parlor. "I'll have Polly bring us some coffee."

"All right, Manda. You don't have to go all formal with me. You know why I'm here. I want to know what you're going to do with four children. How old are they? We knew one was coming, but four? Whose idea was it?"

To Lydia's amazement, Manda burst into tears and covered her face with her hands.

"Land sakes! You can always send them back if you can't handle it. I heard that Edith Watkins wanted one. And Emma Swartz sent Ed in for one. It's not like there's no getting out of it."

Manda shook her head and continued to sob while Lydia watched, unsure whether to take her leave or stay and try to comfort her friend.

"I'll go get the coffee," she decided, and bustled off toward the kitchen.

When she returned, Manda had regained her composure and was jabbing at her eyes with a handkerchief.

"You might as well know. Everybody is going to find out anyway, now that Chad has decided to tell his family."

Lydia listened in disbelief as Manda outlined the year ahead of them.

"He'll get the crops in, then have the winter to get things ready to move. His brother George will run this place while we're gone. Chad has been thinking on this for a long time without letting me know. If I'd had any idea this was coming, we wouldn't have taken the children. But since we did, we'll keep them."

"The Lord has a reason for everything He brings into our lives. He also intends it for our good—although I can't see the good in this," Lydia admitted. "Seems like a mistake to me. Chad has more land now than he can cover in a day. You'd think he'd be satisfied."

Manda nodded. There seemed to be nothing left to say.

Lydia rose and started for the door. "Actually, I came to see the children, but I'll do that another time." She patted Manda's hand and stepped out on the porch. "My, oh my. This is a pretty kettle of fish."

Manda couldn't have agreed more. And she was uncomfortably aware that it was her kettle. There was no time to sit and mull it over. She picked up the coffee cups, straightened her shoulders, and marched toward the kitchen to endure

Polly's thoughts on the subject.

Frances had arisen later than the rest of the family, and was eating her breakfast when Manda appeared. She seemed not to notice that her mother was there. Polly continued with her work, ignoring the fact that anyone else was in her kitchen.

Manda sat down at the table. "I suppose everyone thinks this is all my fault," she said finally.

"I thought it was my fault," Frances said. "I'm the one that wanted you and Papa to get the children from Briarlane."

" 'Tain't no one's fault," Polly put in. "Chad didn't just make up his mind last night to pick up and move. He could have said he had other plans if he'd a mind to. This is one of them things in life that God knows about, and He'll work it out for the best."

"That's what Lydia said," Manda admitted. "But for the life of me, I don't see how."

"Don't have to," Polly declared. "All's we have to do is keep working. If we're going to live out in the wilds of nowhere in a dirt cellar, we better get ready for it. You ever been in a soddy?"

"I have not, and I'd like to keep it that way. Not that anyone asked me, of course. Frances, you watch after the children and keep them busy. I've got to sort out my thinking and make plans."

"Never seen Manda when she wasn't in charge," Polly reported to Luke and Henry at noon. "She ain't never moved all her belongings across the country before. She's plumb baffled."

"She'll come around," Luke predicted. "That's one lady you won't keep down for long. She'll be running the show before the week's out."

Luke was right. In the days that followed, life settled into a routine. The first Sunday after the Coopers arrived, Manda presented a well-turned-out family at the church. She was even able to appear calm in the face of curious questions from fellow parishioners.

"Yes, it's true we're planning to spend a year in South Dakota. No, the children won't be a problem. All but the baby can help some."

"You're a brave woman, Manda, to leave your big house and move out to the prairie. You won't have things so convenient as they are now."

Manda felt anything but brave, but she was determined to make the best of it. If she felt that the situation was slipping out of her hands, no one would ever know it. So she smiled and assured her neighbors that all would be well, and wished fervently that she felt as confident as she appeared.

ETHAN

Ethan paused and looked out the big barn door. His sister Alice was half carrying, half dragging a bucket toward the pig trough. Six years old was too young for such heavy work, he thought. Should he run quickly and help her?

The question was answered by a gruff voice from the hay mow above him.

"You're not going to get the hay moved by leaning on the pitch fork, boy. What are you waiting for?"

Ethan glanced up at the man who spoke, then went back to his work.

"I asked you a question. Are you going to answer me?"

"Yes, sir. I was watching Alice. I thought maybe she needed help."

"She can take care of her own chores," the man said. "You mind your own."

"Yes, sir."

I'm lucky he wasn't down here, Ethan thought. *He probably would have swatted me.* He hurried to finish filling the cow's stalls so that he could escape to the field to work with Luke. It was hotter out there, but at least Luke was friendly.

"You been here awhile now," Luke said when Ethan joined him. "You like this better than the orphanage?"

"It's harder work," Ethan replied, "but I guess that doesn't hurt me. We get good food."

Luke grinned at the boy. "You'll probably be a lawyer someday. You know how to answer a question without answering it." He turned back to his plow, and Ethan followed along behind him, tossing potatoes into the bag he carried.

"Chad Rush is a hard man," Luke continued, "but he runs a good farm. Don't know much about boys, though. 'Course, I can't say as I do either, but I wouldn't knock 'em around."

"He says he's trying to teach me to be a good farmer," Ethan replied. "I guess that's the only way he knows. I couldn't stand to see him hit Simon or Will, though."

"Simon isn't five yet, and Manda will see to it that he doesn't touch Will. You don't need to worry about them." Luke glanced back at the boy. "This is some different from what you expected, I reckon."

Ethan nodded. It was indeed. He remembered what Bert had said as they traveled west on the train. "Every place is about the same. It's the people you have to get used to."

Ethan had gotten used to a lot of people in his nine years. When Ma died, his older brothers sent him and the younger ones to Briarlane, the county orphanage. There he learned how God loved him and would go with him wherever he went. For the first time in his life he made a friend who shared his fears and good times equally. It was a comfort to have Bert as close as he was now, though they saw each other only occasionally.

Luke didn't seem inclined to talk anymore, so Ethan let his mind wander as he followed the plow down the long rows. This was certainly a different kind of place from any he had ever known before. Not only was Chad Rush's farm bigger than he could imagine, he had never known people like Chad and Manda. Ethan recalled the first weekend after their arrival. Following Saturday night supper, Manda had issued directions for the evening.

"Frances, help Alice with her bath and wash her hair. Then Ethan, you take care of the younger boys and have your bath. Be sure all heads are scrubbed, then come to the kitchen."

What followed was endured stoically by all three boys. Manda trimmed nails and Polly wrapped a huge towel around each boy in turn, then proceeded to cut their hair. Luke and Henry sat at the table, awaiting their turn, and offered advice.

"You got that side higher than this one, Polly. You better even it up."

"Whoops! There, you went too high. Now you'll have to take it off the other side again. That boy's not going to have any hair to wear to church tomorrow if you don't watch it."

Simon sat wide-eyed as the scissors snipped around his ears. Hair scratched his neck and slid down inside the towel. He wiggled on the high stool.

"Sit still, Simon," Polly directed him. "You don't want to lose a piece of your ear. And you two keep quiet," she said to the men, "or I'll give a haircut you won't forget for a while."

"We get one of those every month," Luke said. "That won't be nothing new."

Sunday was a day of joy. The household turned out early to ready themselves for church. Manda and Polly packed large picnic baskets, for it was to be an all-day affair.

Simon was awed to learn that Frances played the church organ. "Could I learn to play the organ, Frances?"

"I suppose you could when you get older," she told him. "You have to be big enough to reach the pedals. You'll need to practice awfully hard too."

"Oh, I would. Will you teach me how?"

Frances assured him that she'd try, just as soon as he grew taller. Simon wasn't willing to wait that long.

"I'll sit on your lap, and you can pedal while I play the notes. Then when I'm big enough to play alone, I'll know how to do it."

Frances laughed at the little boy's enthusiasm and promised that they would try it sometime.

Ethan waited impatiently for the buggy to stop in the churchyard. His first project was to find Bert.

Even though Bert lived far out on the prairie with his new parents, Ethan was sure that they would be in town for church. He was not disappointed. Bert was standing with Carl and Hannah Boncoeur, and when he spotted Ethan, he ran toward him with a whoop of delight. The two boys pounded each other on the back and would have scuffled in the dusty yard had it not been for their Sunday clothes and the watchful eye of Polly. They were allowed to sit together during the church service, as long as they didn't whisper. Ethan couldn't resist pointing out that the girl at the organ was his new sister, Frances.

When church was over, the families gathered to share food and conversation. The Rushes were surrounded by neighbors who wanted to see the children from the Orphan Train.

"Why is everyone staring at us?" Simon wanted to know.

"Because we just came," Ethan told him. "They don't know us yet."

After they had all been asked names, ages, and grades in school, attention turned from the Coopers to Chad and Manda.

Bert and Ethan were pleased to be turned loose and to be able to go and sit by the river to talk. They dangled their feet in the water as Bert happily related to Ethan the joys of prairie life.

"Remember the little town where we left Riley off and you couldn't see some of the houses? That's the kind of place we have. Right now it's all underground, but Papa says we're going to build a real house next spring."

"If it's all underground, where did they put the

windows?" Ethan wanted to know.

"There aren't any windows, but there's a big door that lets in air and light. There's a chimney that takes the smoke out from the stove."

"I guess you like your folks, huh?"

Bert grinned widely. "I sure do. My mama laughs and sings and cooks great food. She brought lots of pretty things with her from Louisiana, and you know what? She had a room with bright red curtains for walls fixed up for me before I even got there!"

"Do you help your papa in the fields?"

"Every day. He says he doesn't know how he ever ran the place without me. 'Course, he teases a lot. I think he did pretty good before I came."

Bert tossed a few pebbles into the water before he continued. "You know, I never thought I'd be this lucky. When we were there in Briarlane, I pretended that my real folks would come back for me, but I guess I knew they wouldn't. I'd have stayed there until I was sixteen like Hugh did, then gone out to work somewhere if it hadn't been for the Orphan Train. Matron was right when she said the Lord had a place for us. He sure picked a good one for me!"

"You going to come in here to school when it opens?" Ethan asked.

Bert nodded. "Yep. Papa says I can ride Trotter to school. Trotter's used to me now, 'cause I ride him a lot. You got horses on your farm?"

"Four of them."

"Do you get to ride one?"

"No, they're for work, Chad says. He doesn't even want us to talk to them."

Bert couldn't understand this. "Our horses work, and we talk to them all the time. Can't you talk to any of the animals?"

Ethan shook his head. "Chad doesn't like talking much. He says it takes your mind off your work. I talk to Luke and Henry some, but not when Chad is around."

Bert turned this over in his mind, then he ventured, "Don't you even call your folks Mama and Papa?"

"Will and Simon do, but that's because they're younger. Alice and I are old enough to face the facts of life, Manda says. I kind of feel like they aren't really being our parents; they're just keeping us."

"Maybe they'll get to like you so much that they'll turn into your parents," Bert suggested. "They just don't know you very well yet. Do you have a nice house to live in?"

Here Ethan was on firm ground. "Remember the Quincys' house back in Briarlane? It's almost as big as that. Alice has a room next to Frances, and Simon and I have a bedroom across the hall. Will sleeps in a little room next to Chad and Manda." Ethan paused and thought a moment. "I think Manda likes Will best."

The boys sat quietly and watched the bugs hover over the water. Finally Bert broke the silence.

"I guess you're not very happy, huh?"

"Maybe not as much as you are," Ethan admitted, "but I'm not awful unhappy. We're all together, and we get lots of good food. Manda already made two new dresses for Alice and shirts for Simon and Will. There is one thing I'm kinda worried about, though."

Bert was silent, and Ethan went on.

"The first night we were there Chad said we were moving to South Dakota in the spring. But I don't know if 'we' includes us Coopers. No one has said a word about it since, so maybe Manda changed his mind. I just don't know. Anyway, I'll be going to school with you this year. I heard Chad say I could go as soon as work was done in the fields."

Bert was indignant. "I'd rather live in a soddy with somebody who wanted me than in a house with lots of rooms where nobody cared whether I was there or not!"

"Oh, I think they care," Ethan said. "It's just that they might not have known how many four more children were all at once. We'll get along fine once they're used to us."

Bert wasn't sure about that, but he couldn't think of anything comforting to say to his friend. There was no more chance to talk, since it was time to start for home and take care of the chores.

"I'll see you next Sunday, Ethan. I'll ask my folks if you can come out and visit me. You can ride Trotter and see our spread."

Ethan's face brightened at the suggestion, and all the way home he dreamed about the open prairie and a soddy with bright red curtains. He would work hard during the coming week so that Chad wouldn't have a reason to refuse the invitation.

"Certainly not," Chad said when Ethan got up enough

courage to ask him. "What makes you think we have time around here to play? Doubt I'll be able to get you into shape to be any use on the new place. Forget about going off visiting."

That was a long speech for Chad, but at least Ethan knew that plans were made for them to go with the family. He resolved to prove that he could do anything that was asked of him.

But as the summer went on, it seemed harder and harder to please Chad. If Ethan had to be told more than once how to do something, the instruction was accompanied by a strapping. If he didn't work fast enough, he was punished.

Luke ventured to protest Chad's harshness with the boy.

"It's none of your business, Luke," Chad replied. "It's my duty to teach him how to work. Someday part of the land will be his. I don't intend to throw it away on a good-for-nothing man. My pa taught me how to prosper, and I intend to teach these boys."

Luke repeated this conversation to Henry and added his own conclusions. "I think Chad has met up with a boy who has as much gumption as he had. It will be hard for Chad to give up until he breaks Ethan—just as his pa tried to do with him. I'm wagering that the kid will hold out. He's a strong one."

Henry nodded. "He also has a strong faith in God. That will keep him going."

"You could be right, but so far I can't see as his faith has done him any favors. I'm going to help him all I can."

Although Ethan was unaware of the men's concern for him, he was thankful for their friendship. Working with Luke or Henry was a pleasure, because Ethan really did enjoy farming.

Now, hauling potatoes back to the root cellar, Ethan wondered what the new homestead would be like. They had passed a lot of desolate-looking prairie on the train trip west. Would there be buffalo? He remembered that Chad had mentioned an Indian reservation. Would they see the Indians? Would they be friendly?

He wouldn't have long to wait, Ethan thought. Summer was almost over, and soon school would begin. He looked forward to that, since he could see Bert every day and there would be time to read and draw. Frances had told him that he'd have a lady schoolteacher this year.

Yes, life was pretty good, Ethan decided. God had found the right place for him, too.

BEGINNING
THE MOVE

In late August Chad announced that he and Henry would be leaving for South Dakota the following week. The news was received with tears from Frances, grim silence from Manda, and curious questions from the younger children.

"Will you see the Indians?" Simon wanted to know.

"We might," Chad replied. "Our land is just outside the reservation. We're going to find a place near the river to put our house."

"This house?" Alice asked. "Will this house move to South Dakota?"

"Of course not, Alice." Simon answered the question. "They have to build a new one up there, don't they, Papa?"

Chad nodded. "We'll get the cellar dug and build a shelter for the animals. The house and barn will be built after we move."

"I'll go and help," Simon declared. "I know how to dig."

"You'll stay here," Ethan told him. "You'd be in the way when they're trying to work. You can help Luke and me in the barn."

Simon scowled, but he didn't say anymore about it. He watched carefully as the wagons were loaded with tools, building materials, and camping gear.

Polly was kept busy baking and preparing food for them to take on the trip. Dried meat, vegetables that wouldn't spoil in the heat, and canned goods were packed in the wagon. Simon was allowed to go into town with Henry to have the horses shod for the trip. He was eager to share the experience when he returned.

"You know what the smithy did?" he asked Alice.

"What's a smithy?"

"A blacksmith," Simon explained patiently. "He has a big fire, and he puts these horseshoes into it until they're red hot, then he dunks 'em in a barrel, and they go f-z-z-z, and smoke comes out."

Alice's eyes were wide with horror. "He burned the horses' feet? Why did Henry let him do that?"

"I didn't say he burned the horses' feet!" Simon shouted. "They didn't even have the shoes on yet! It's no use trying to tell a girl anything."

Simon turned away in disgust, but Alice ran after him. "Tell me, Simon! Tell me what he did next. I won't say anything more."

"Well, all right. Then the smithy put the shoe on a big iron table and banged it with a hammer until it was the right size. Then he picked up Ned's foot and fastened the shoe on with big nails."

Alice gasped. "Nails in his foot?" Then she remembered her promise and clapped her hands over her mouth.

Simon didn't choose to admit that he had reacted the same way, so he answered patiently.

"It didn't hurt him. Henry said Ned's hooves are too thick to feel the nails. In fact, Ned likes his new shoes, and so does Jesse."

Simon left for the barn to keep an eye on the preparations, and Alice sat down on the back step. She was lonely. At Briarlane there had been little girls to play with, especially Betsy, who had guided her through the routines of the orphanage and her first year at school. Betsy was the only friend Alice had ever had who was her own age, but Betsy had found a new family on one of the first stops the Orphan Train made.

Simon had always been glad to play with Alice before, but now the marvels of the farm took him off to the fields or the barn in pursuit of Luke or Henry or Ethan.

Ethan. Her big brother had always looked after her and made sure that she was safe. But since they had come to the Rushes, Alice saw Ethan only at meal times. And if he didn't finish his chores fast enough or well enough, he had to eat in the kitchen rather than with the family.

Alice sighed and drew circles in the dirt with her toe. This was her home, and she was glad that her brothers were here with her, but she did wish that Manda could be more like Matron. No one but Will had been hugged since they came here. Alice thought that Manda would probably be happier if she had only Will to take care of.

She did have a big sister now, Alice reflected. Frances was kind to her, and after the first few days, began to pay attention to the one little girl in this group of strange children. One day they had gone together to pick wild strawberries.

"Here, Alice. Polly needs some berries for supper. Do you want to help pick them?" Frances handed Alice a lard pail, and they walked together to the fence at the edge of the road. Frances helped her over, and Alice skipped to keep up with her as they headed for the berry bushes.

"Does your papa own all these berries, too?" Alice asked.

"Yes, he owns everything you can see." Frances plopped the berries into her bucket so hard that some of them bounced out. "That ought to be enough for him. This place is good enough for me, and I don't want to go to South Dakota. Mama doesn't either, but when Papa makes up his mind, that's what we do."

Frances sat down on the grass and pulled her knees up under her chin. Alice sat down beside her. They gazed off over the fields for a moment.

"I lived in Briarlane when I was younger, just like you did," Frances said.

"You did? I don't remember seeing you."

"It was a long time ago. You weren't even born yet. I was just your age when I came here."

"Did you come on an Orphan Train?"

Frances shook her head. "No, Mama and Papa came to

Hull House in Chicago to get me and my baby brother. We traveled out here on a train, but it wasn't an Orphan Train."

"I didn't know you had a baby brother, Frances. Where is he now?"

"He died of pneumonia. That's why Mama likes Will so much. He reminds her of Robbie." Frances jumped to her feet. "We'd better finish these berries and get back to the house. Polly will be after us."

"I like Polly," Alice said. "She lets me help bake."

"I know. I used to help when I was little too. Since I'm in school and have to practice the organ, I don't have much time. She's lucky to have you." Frances smiled at the little girl, and they returned to their job. The pails were soon full, and they headed for home.

Recalling that day, Alice wished that she and Frances could do more things together, but Frances and Manda were busy sewing for the family. Alice got up and wandered out toward the barn to see what was being done for the trip. Ethan said the men were leaving early in the morning.

Polly and Manda scurried around the kitchen in last-minute preparation for the departure.

"We'll pack their dinner for tomorrow so they won't have to stop until nightfall," Manda directed. "When Chad is ready to go, he doesn't want anything to get in his way."

"He wouldn't be so eager to go if he had to do all the gettin' ready," Polly declared. "Who knows how long it will take them to get there—let alone do all that work? How are we going to pack these eggs?"

"Have Ethan fill this wooden box with sawdust," Manda decided. "The eggs will ride in that."

"They're going to get mighty tired of rustling their own meals after they've dug all day," Polly said. "I'm surprised he didn't have one of us go along."

"He knew better than to ask me," Manda replied, "and I wouldn't be able to manage here without you. They'll just have to do the best they can."

The women worked in silence for a few minutes, then Polly brought up another topic that had been bothering her.

"This here soddy. How big do you reckon it will be?"

"Not big enough for all of us to live in like human beings," Manda snapped. "I never thought I'd see the day that I'd take all my belongings and set up house in a hole in the ground. The best we can hope for is that they'll find a suitable spot by the river. No telling how long it will be until we have a well."

Polly wiped her face with her apron. "It's bound to be cooler underground in the summer than it is in this kitchen." She pulled the pies from the oven and set them on the table. "Cherry, apple, blueberry, and rhubarb. That should hold them for a few days."

By suppertime Chad pronounced the big wagon loaded and ready to go.

"We'll leave by four in the morning," he said. "That should get us to the Niobrara River by night."

When Ethan rose to follow Luke to the barn the next morning, the wagon was gone.

"How long do you suppose they'll be away?"

"Longer than Chad thinks, unless he gets someone to help them," Luke replied. "My guess is he'll hire some Indians to work, once he decides where the house will go."

Ethan couldn't imagine pulling up in the middle of the vast prairie and building a house, and he said as much to Luke.

"Lots of folks has done it. Chad was smart enough to stake a claim along the Cottonwood Creek, so water is one less worry he'll have. He won't have no house up right away, I can tell you that. The barn will come first."

"Will we take any animals?"

"Just a few milk cows and a couple pigs. George will be running this place, so Chad will take only what he needs to get started. It will be easy to get stock up there. Easier than moving all these." Luke gently whacked the last cow through the fence to the pasture and closed the gate. Together they separated the milk and headed for the house.

"Took longer this morning without Henry helping, but you did a good job, Ethan. You're going to make a good farmer."

Ethan beamed at the compliment. That was exactly what he wanted to do. Maybe one day he'd have a place of his own.

Polly greeted them at the door. "Hurry and wash up. The rest of the family's already eating. 'Tain't as if I didn't have enough to do today without running a late dining room for the three of you."

Luke looked up from the wash basin in surprise.

"Three of us? Henry's gone. There's just Ethan and me."

Polly stepped to the door and looked out toward the barn. "How come you didn't bring Simon with you? Is he out there playing in the barn?"

"Simon wasn't with us."

"He can't be asleep this late," Polly said. "He's always afraid he'll miss something. Ethan, run up and get him down here. Goodness knows I'm not going to be serving meals all day."

Ethan sped up to the room he shared with Simon, but the little boy's bed was empty.

"He's not there," Ethan reported. "He's probably playing down by the creek. He asked me to go fishing some day."

"Well, go ahead and eat your breakfast. He'll come when he gets hungry. Not that I'm going to stop my work to feed him. He can gnaw on a corn cob like the prodigal son."

Luke winked at Ethan. They both knew that Polly had a soft heart when it came to the children, no matter how much she complained.

Manda had other things on her mind at breakfast, so it never occurred to her that Simon wasn't eating in the kitchen with Luke and Ethan. She looked around the dining room and thoughtfully eyed each piece of furniture. The heavy oak table sat in the middle of the floor, surrounded by ten massive chairs. Along one wall was the sideboard containing her good dishes. An armoire full of table linens and scarves stood at the far end. The windows were resplendent with heavy velour drapes, and the pictures on the walls in their large, cumbersome frames made an elegant room.

How much would she be allowed to take with her? Certainly not all of it. What space could she expect to have in a one-room soddy? And what would the damp underground atmosphere do to it? Manda wrinkled her nose at the thought of her good quilts and bedclothes growing mildewed from lack of sunlight. The only thing that cellar would be good for was root vegetables, apples, and canned food, as far as she was concerned.

But, as Lydia said, the Lord had a purpose for all this, even if He hadn't revealed it to her. Manda rose from the table and tackled the huge mound of sewing that awaited her.

At dinnertime Polly carried fried chicken and mashed potatoes into the dining room. Manda, Alice, and Will were taking their places at the table.

"Where's Simon?" Polly asked.

"I haven't seen him," Frances replied. "I thought he was eating out there with you."

"Well, he's not." She didn't add that he hadn't been there for breakfast, either. Preoccupied with all she had to do, Polly had forgotten that she hadn't seen the little boy all morning. "Alice, was he with you?"

"No, I went to the creek with Will. We didn't see him."

Polly slammed the dishes down harder than necessary and muttered, "I have enough to do around here without keeping track of three extra young ones. He'd better get in here with Ethan, or he's in trouble."

But Simon didn't appear with Luke and Ethan, nor had they seen him all morning.

"Eat your dinner, then you set out and find him," Polly said to Ethan. "I'm going to tan him good for running off without telling anyone."

Polly was frightened. Not only had Simon endeared himself to her, but she remembered too vividly the sadness in this house when Robbie had died. What if something happened to this little boy too?

When a search of the barn, the creek, and the near fields revealed no Simon, Polly approached Manda in the upstairs sewing room.

"We can't find Simon."

"It's not time for supper yet," Manda murmured around a mouthful of pins.

"We haven't seen him all day."

Manda removed the pins. "You mean he hasn't been in since breakfast?"

"He wasn't here for breakfast."

Manda dropped her scissors and sprang to her feet. "Why didn't you tell me before? Is Luke searching for him?"

"Has been, ever since dinnertime. Everyone thought he was with someone else this morning. I was sure they'd find him right away."

Manda ran down the stairs and out to the porch. Frances and Alice, with Will between them, were coming up the lane.

"He's not down by the berry bushes," Frances reported, "and he's not on the road either way, as far as we could see."

"Simon went in a car?" Will asked, tugging at Ethan's shirt.

"No, Will, I don't think so. Simon is big enough not to go off with someone he doesn't know."

"There's no car around here for him to go in," Luke said. "He used another way to get off the farm, or else he's still here somewhere."

"Simon said he was going with Henry," Alice ventured.

"Yes! He did!" Ethan looked at Luke. "I told him he couldn't because—"

Before Ethan could finish the sentence, Luke was racing toward the barn. A few minutes later, the buggy was headed north to the Niobrara River.

5

An Unexpected
Trip

Chad and Henry rode in silence through the early morning darkness, each absorbed in his own thoughts. The breeze was cool, giving no hint of the sweltering August day that lay ahead of them. Chad reviewed in his mind what had been packed, and planned how he would choose the spot for their future house. He had been fortunate to lay claim to 460 acres along the Cottonwood Creek, which was fed by the White River to the north. There would be abundant water, and he'd have no problem finding building material. He envisioned a soddy about twenty by twenty feet that would house his family until construction could begin on a permanent home.

Henry interrupted Chad's thought. "What's the nearest town to your land?"

"Place called Winner, to the east a ways," Chad replied. "That's where the train will come in with our goods and the family."

"No place like Willow Creek that's easy to get to, then."

"Not that I know of. Our closest neighbors will be the Indians. Might be a few homesteaders on up north, but I don't know of any nearby." Chad glanced at Henry. "I'm thinking of filing for another section along the river. If you and Luke each lay claim to a section, we'll have good pasture. We could run a good herd on 2,500 acres of prairie."

"How much do you figure a section would cost?"

"Last I heard, about $1.25 an acre—that would be $800.00."

Henry was skeptical. "Where would Luke and me get that kind of money?"

"You won't need it," Chad told him. "You file the claim in your name and transfer it to me. I'll pay for the land. From what I hear, choice property up there is going to be hard to come by soon. The further you get from the water, the harder it is to farm or run cattle." Chad was warming to his subject. "Cattle will be a good investment. We can ship them on down to Omaha, and the Rock Island Railway will take them into Chicago. As I see it, we can't lose."

Henry considered this information as the sun rose higher. The heat and dusty road made traveling uncomfortable, and they were glad to stop at dinnertime to rest and water the horses. While the team grazed, Chad and Henry lay in the shade by the stream with their hats over their faces. They didn't see or hear the little boy who climbed out of the wagon to eat the leftovers from their meal and wade in the cool water.

Luke paced the horse as he started out in the hot afternoon. When the sun went down in a few hours, he would let the mare go at her own speed. Dancer was one of Chad's best runners, and given about four hours of twilight after sunset, they should reach the heavily loaded wagon by dark.

Luke wasn't much dependent on prayer in his life. He attended church regularly with the family, and good-naturedly accepted the frequent suggestions from Henry that he should consider the needs of his soul.

"Yep. I probably should. My ma's been telling me too, but look how old she is. I have a lot of years ahead of me before I need to get serious about religion."

"You don't have any guarantee on how long you'll live," Henry reminded him. "I've known folks younger than you who've met their Maker."

"I guess unless I get kicked in the head by a horse or you run me over with the threshing machine, I'll take my chances. You just keep on praying for me, and I'll be safe."

Now as the sun set and the air began to cool, Luke's mind started to wander. He recalled the day that Frances and Robbie had been brought home by the Rushes. Robbie was a little towhead, still in rompers. Every chance he found to escape from Frances or Manda, he would follow after Luke. Robbie's delight in being allowed to ride to the barn on a load of hay or sit on the broad back of a work horse pleased Luke. When Robbie died tragically after an illness, the big man grieved along with the family. What good, Luke reflected, had everyone's prayers done then?

Nevertheless, Luke found himself wishing that he knew a little something about praying as he followed the lonely country road north. He was sure he was on the track of the missing Simon, but if the little boy had hidden on the wagon, and neither Chad nor Henry had discovered him, how could he have survived the day? It wasn't likely that Simon had thought to take food or water. Could he live long in the intense heat without them?

"Lord," Luke said out loud, "I'm not asking for me, because I know I ain't worthy of Your notice, but that little boy is in trouble. I'd feel better if I thought You was looking out for him. Seems like Chad and Manda couldn't stand to lose another young one. If You ever listen to the likes of me, I'd be mighty grateful. Thank You."

Somehow Luke felt comforted after praying, and his spirits lifted. After a short stop to rest and water the horse, and eat the biscuits and ham he had quickly snatched from the kitchen, he refilled his canteen and headed Dancer north again. He should reach the others shortly after dark.

The Niobrara River, Chad's destination for the night, was barely visible in the semidarkness, but the men could hear the rushing water as they approached. It had been a long, tiring day, and they were glad to stop at last.

"Too dark now to see where we can cross in the morning," Chad remarked as he unhitched the team from the wagon. "Ed Swartz says we won't have trouble if we're near a place called Meadville. Not too far off this road, he says."

The horses were tethered for a well-earned rest, and the men set up camp. While Henry pulled the bed rolls from the back of the wagon, Chad built a fire and prepared to heat the stew that Polly had sent for the evening meal. Stars were starting to appear, and the night promised to be a clear one.

"How far you reckon we have to go yet?" Henry asked.

"We're over halfway now, not too far from the border."

"Not very well populated, is it?"

"Nope." Chad poked the fire and sent sparks flying skyward. "Mostly buffalo and antelope and Indians. We're pretty much on our own."

The horses lifted their heads, and Ned whinnied.

Chad stood up. "We're having company."

Moments later the clop of a horse's hooves could be heard plainly, and the men waited for the appearance of whoever was on the road at this time of night.

When Luke jumped down from the buggy, Chad grabbed his arm. "What's happened? Is something wrong at home?"

Luke peered anxiously around in the darkness before he answered. "I was sure he snuck out with you. Where else could he be?"

Chad shook his arm. "Who, man? Where could who be?"

"Simon," Luke replied. And while Henry unhitched and fed Dancer, Luke told the men of the day's events.

"Everyone thought he was with someone else—that's why I'm so late catching up with you. Then Alice remembered that Simon had said he was coming with you, so I was certain this was where he'd be. I sure don't want to go back and tell the others that Simon isn't here."

Henry ladled out a dish of stew for Luke and handed him a hunk of corn bread. Both men watched Chad's stern face in the firelight.

"We'll have to head back in the morning," Chad decided. "Manda won't get over it if we lose another boy."

"You can't just 'lose' a boy off a place as big as ours," Luke reasoned. "Where would he have gone? He's only five."

A small voice brought all three men to their feet. "I'm hungry."

Chad lifted Simon and set him in front of the fire. "Where did you come from?"

Simon pointed to the wagon. "I been riding in there. I got hungry. You didn't leave much dinner for me today," he said accusingly.

"I ought to strap you good," Chad told him. "You've worried your mama half to death and scared the whole family. Whatever got into you?"

The little boy's lip quivered. "I wanted to help. I know how to dig."

"You were told that you couldn't come. You aren't old enough to do that kind of work."

"Ethan told me I couldn't," Simon replied, "but you didn't. I thought you wanted me."

Henry quickly thrust a piece of corn bread into Simon's hand and scrubbed out a plate for his stew.

"What I want to know is why you didn't suffocate or die of the heat in that wagon," Luke said. "Where'd you ride, anyway?"

"By the ice," Simon answered around a mouthful of bread. "I licked it off. But I couldn't get the food stuff opened."

"That's what saved his life," Henry declared. "We stuffed a cake of ice into a gunny sack this morning and put it in last thing. Thought it would keep the food fresher for a few days. He never would have made it otherwise. The Lord was looking after you, boy."

"The Lord's got His work cut out for Him when you get back home and Manda gets hold of you," Luke chuckled. "You're going to need protection from somewhere."

A lonesome-sounding howl filled the air, and the horses stomped their feet and flicked their ears.

"Timber wolf," Chad said. "Lots of those out here. Coyotes, too. They'll be around in the night."

"Will they get us?" Simon inquired anxiously.

"Nope. We'll keep the fire going all night. They won't come close to fire. Time to turn in. We've got a long journey ahead tomorrow."

They were soon rolled up in their blankets, and the only sounds were the rustling wind in the trees and the water rushing by. If silent eyes observed them during the night, the sleepers didn't know it.

At the Rushes' farm, it was a quiet group who came to breakfast the next morning. Although they didn't expect Luke to return until later in the day, the strain of waiting showed on them.

Polly and Manda helped Ethan with the milking and

chores in the absence of all three men. Then Polly hovered around the dining room table as if reluctant to stay in her empty kitchen alone with her thoughts.

"You haven't eaten yet, Polly," Manda stated. "Set your place out here and have your breakfast."

Frances looked up at her mother in surprise. This was an unusual gesture.

Manda was pale and looked as though she hadn't slept well. She glanced around the table at the children.

Ethan had scarcely touched his food, and he kept looking toward the big window. This was the second time that he had lost sight of Simon since Ma had urged him to look after the little ones, just before she died. Why hadn't he noticed that Simon was gone before he left for the barn yesterday? Or had Simon even been there the night before? Ethan didn't know. In both instances, Ethan recalled, he had not noticed that Simon was missing until long after he was gone, first on the Orphan Train west, and now here. Perhaps Chad was right. He needed to have some responsibility knocked into him. After all, he would be ten years old in November.

Frances broke into his thoughts. "Don't worry, Ethan. Luke will find him. And it wasn't your fault. None of us checked to be sure where he was all day."

Ethan smiled at her gratefully.

Only Will seemed blissfully unaware of the concern around him. He spooned mush and milk into his mouth, then tackled a huge piece of bread and jam, chattering all the while. Alice tried to answer his questions, but her attention really wasn't on her small brother. She wished that Matron were there to comfort them with a Bible verse.

As though reading Alice's thoughts too, Frances said, "Let's say the Twenty-third Psalm together, since Papa isn't here to read the Scripture." They did, and Manda prayed a short prayer for the safety of Luke and Simon.

Manda was unusually quiet as she worked with Polly to begin the fall canning. Though she would not have admitted it, even to her good friend Lydia, Manda wished that she knew the Lord better. The past few months had shown her that she was going to need more than her own wisdom to raise these children as she should. Frances had not been a problem, even though she was headstrong, and Chad was inclined to be lenient with her. She was a tenderhearted, unselfish girl, and Manda had never had cause to worry about her ability in school or in music.

These new children were still unknown to her. They were quiet and obedient, and up to now, she'd had no problems that were not easy to solve. Simon's disappearance had shaken her, though, and Manda felt that she wasn't close enough to the Lord to depend on Him as she would like to have done. Perhaps they needed to think about making their Christian profession a more important part of their lives. Manda determined to talk with Chad about it as soon as he was home again.

It was a tired little boy who returned home with Luke late that afternoon. Manda was so relieved to see him that she had him in her arms before he could reach the porch. Ethan stared in surprise. Manda had cared well for them, but she had never shown affection to any of the children except Will. Even as he prepared a lecture for his little brother, Ethan hoped that this unexpected tenderness would continue.

Both Luke and Polly ate supper with the family that evening, for everyone wanted to hear about the adventure.

"The wagon was bumpy, and I got hungry," Simon told them. "And we heard coyotes and timber woofs."

"Wolves," Luke corrected. "There are a lot of them on the prairie."

"Do they bite?" This question came from Alice.

"As a general rule they stay away from humans," Luke answered. "They come around when food is scarce, but they aren't likely to attack people. They'll sneak up and get what they can to eat, then leave."

It wasn't late when everyone retired that night. It had been a hard day for all of them. As Ethan watched Simon sleeping soundly in his own bed, he recalled the story of the lost sheep that Matron had told them at Briarlane. Luke had been the shepherd for Simon, and Ethan was grateful to his friend. He would work especially hard tomorrow to thank him.

6

THE KEY

Ethan hunched over his desk and chewed the end of his pencil. He could hear rustling and noise around him, but he didn't look up to see what was going on. He had learned soon after school began that the less he appeared to notice, the better off he was.

Going to school in Briarlane had been different. All the children at the Christian Children's Home had gone together, and no one had thought about their being orphans. But here in Willow Creek, he and Bert and Alice were "Orphan Train Kids," and they weren't allowed to forget it. No mistake was overlooked, and no difference escaped the notice of the town children.

Ethan had hoped to make new friends at school; instead he felt as though he didn't belong.

"I think we'd get along better without Hector," Bert said. "He's the one who keeps reminding everyone that we came off the street. I'd like to poke him in the eye."

"I don't think that would be a good idea," Ethan replied. "Most everyone does what Hector tells them to. I'm just going to stay out of his way."

Ethan did try to avoid the older boy, but it wasn't always possible. As soon as Frances and Alice joined the girls on the school ground, Hector and his friends would surround Ethan and Bert.

"Are you sure you ever been to school before?" Hector would ask. "How come you don't know how to multiply and divide? Did you guys hear the answers he gave this morning? Are all orphans as dumb as you are?"

Once in a while another boy would stand up for them. "Aw, leave them alone, Hector. They can't help it if their folks died."

Ethan hoped that no one would ever find out that his pa hadn't died, but had gone off and left them. He didn't want them to think that even his own pa couldn't stand him.

Chad and Henry had returned from the homestead shortly after school began. They reported that the soddy was ready, as were a shelter for the animals and a bunkhouse for the men. Henry had a little more to tell Luke and Polly.

"You never saw such open space in your life. Nothing but prairie grass as far as you can see. The only green sight is right along the Cottonwood Creek where we're settling. Every day we saw buffalo grazing, and antelope all over the place. Lots of coyote and wolves, too."

"Are you building right near the water?" This was Polly's main concern.

"Yep. Far enough back so that we won't get flooded out in the spring, but close enough to be handy."

"Indians?"

"Lots of 'em. You was right, Luke. Chad hired some of them to help dig. Friendly. Their village is over east of the creek. Reckon we'll see them pretty regular. They offered to dress out any buffalo we shoot in return for the skins."

"Guess maybe we can stand to rough it for a year or so," Polly said. "Never thought I'd be a pioneer at my age. 'Course, I never thought I'd have four more young 'uns to look after either. Seem to be getting along all right with that."

As the school year went on, Ethan found that he did have some friends beside Bert among his schoolmates. There were games during recess and noon hour, and as both boys proved to be top ball players, they were always chosen first when teams were formed.

It wasn't long until Mrs. Finch, their teacher, discovered how well Ethan could draw.

"Ethan, did you do this picture of the school? Have you drawn some other things?"

"He can draw anything he sees," Bert boasted. "I've got a whole drawing book of stuff he did."

Mrs. Finch soon had Ethan putting scenes on the board, or illustrating the science or history lessons. Ethan was pleased to have his work admired. There were times when he could forget about Hector and enjoy school.

At the end of November, Bert was kept at home by heavy snows and cold. Ethan missed having his friend there every day. Since this was the last year for Frances, Manda saw to it that the children did not miss school even when the weather was harsh. Luke would load the sleigh with buffalo robes and warm bricks, and the children would wrap themselves in warm caps and scarves and mittens. When the day was ended, Henry would come to pick them up.

But just when Ethan concluded that things had changed for the better at school, disaster struck.

He reached into his pocket one morning to get a handkerchief, and pulled out the key and chain that Bert had given to him. It clattered to the floor, and before Ethan could bend to get it, Hector had snatched it up and stuffed it in his pocket.

"Give that back!" Ethan whispered. "That's mine."

"Yeah? It's mine now. You probably stole it anyway."

"Is something wrong, boys?" Mrs. Finch looked in their direction.

"No, ma'am," Hector answered. "I just dropped something."

Ethan could say nothing more until school was let out at noon. He approached Hector as soon as he could.

"I want my key back, Hector."

"What ya gonna do if I don't give it to you? Run and tell the teacher?"

Hector removed the big key from his pocket and looked

at it, holding it out of Ethan's reach.

"What does it open?"

"Nothing."

"So what good is a key that don't open nothing? You don't need it anyway." Hector dropped the key back into his pocket and walked off with the other boys.

Ethan felt tears of anger in his eyes. Hector knew that he wouldn't be a telltale.

Ethan would never let anyone know what the key meant to him. Not only had it been Bert's prize possession, freely given to Ethan, it had been a constant reminder that he could pray, and he need never give up, because God would help him. Now it was gone. Somehow he would have to get it back before Bert returned to school. If only there were someone that Ethan might tell who could help him. He knew it would not be wise to speak of it at home. Frances would be sympathetic, but there was nothing she could do.

In December the school began to get ready for the community Christmas celebration. Ethan was given the task of drawing the manger scene on the side blackboard. The teacher produced colored chalks for him to work with, and Ethan didn't think he had ever been so happy in his life. Every spare moment from his studies he labored over Mary, Joseph, and baby Jesus. He could hardly wait to get to school each morning. Day by day, as the children watched, the animals, shepherds, and wise men appeared. The hills, the star, and the angels were added.

The week before the program, everyone arrived to find that someone had smeared the center of the picture. Mary, Joseph, and baby Jesus were gone. Ethan stared at the scene in horror. Who could have done such a thing?

Mrs. Finch was pale with anger. When all the children had taken their seats, she stood behind her desk and looked at each one silently. Finally she spoke.

"Nothing like this has ever happened in our school. I'm not going to ask who did it. I don't want to know who of my students would be guilty of such a terrible act. We will ask Ethan to repair the drawing. If anyone so much as touches a finger to it again, there will be no Christmas celebration in Willow Creek this year. Is that understood?"

Heads nodded.

"Open your books and proceed with your studies."

The room was deathly quiet as Ethan returned to the board to redo the picture. The joy he had felt in being able to produce a thing of beauty was gone. It would look as good as new when finished, but the thought that someone disliked him enough to want to ruin his work saddened him.

Frances tried to comfort Ethan as they rode home that afternoon. "Someone is jealous because you do such beautiful drawings. Don't worry. I'm sure they won't touch it again. No one wants to miss the Christmas celebration."

Ethan was sure he knew who had done it. He wished he could tell Frances about Hector and the key and his suspicions, but that wouldn't be right. He didn't know that Hector had done it, but he couldn't think of anyone else who would be so mean. He would do his best to repair the damage and say nothing.

The entire family came to the celebration, and Ethan beamed with pleasure when Chad said, "Good work, boy." Frances played the piano while everyone sang carols, and Alice spoke a piece by herself.

"Manda seemed mighty pleased with her family," Luke remarked the next morning. "She was as friendly as I've ever seen her."

Polly agreed. "Manda's had a change of heart since them children has been here. Seems like she's more thoughtful and a little more patient."

"They've been good for all of us," Henry put in. "Chad's got a lot on his mind right now, but I think he goes a little easier on Ethan. That, or the boy's learned how to please him."

It was a surprise then, when Chad decided that Ethan would not return to school after Christmas.

"I'm going to need you around here. There's only three months before we leave for South Dakota, and there are lots of jobs to be done."

Manda looked at Chad and said quietly, "I think Ethan should finish his winter term. We can do without his help for another three weeks."

Chad made no reply, but when school began in January, Ethan was allowed to go.

Not only was he glad to see Bert again, but Ethan had

another surprise waiting for him. Hector stood watching as the younger boys pelted each other with snowballs. Just before time to go inside, he called to Ethan.

"Hey, kid, come here. I got something for you."

Reluctantly Ethan walked over to Hector.

"Here's your key. I decided you could have it back." He tossed the key at Ethan and disappeared into the schoolroom.

Ethan dropped the key into his pocket and followed Hector inside. He was puzzled. Was the older boy trying to make up for ruining the picture without admitting that he had done it? Or was Ethan mistaken, and someone else was to blame? Whatever Hector's reason, Ethan was relieved and pleased to have the key and chain back again.

His pleasure didn't last long. Chad, Luke, and Ethan were finishing the evening chores when a large man appeared in the barn door.

"Evening, Oscar. What brings you out here?"

"I come about that there orphan you got living with you."

Ethan paused in his work and listened. The man was Hector's father. What had Ethan done that was bad enough to send Mr. Price after him?"

Chad stepped to the door. "Which one? I have five children here."

"I don't care about the young 'uns nor Frances. I want to see the boy that's in school. My storage cupboard where I keep money until I bank it was opened and cleaned out. It weren't broken into—the thief used a key. My boy tells me that this here orphan was showing a key around at school and boasting about what he'd do."

"Ethan."

Ethan went to stand beside Chad.

"Do you have a key?"

"Yes, sir."

Chad held out his hand, and Ethan dug the key from his pocket.

"There. See?" said Oscar Price triumphantly. He seemed to feel that his case was proven.

Chad turned the key over and looked at it carefully. "Where did you get this?"

"A friend gave it to me. A friend from Briarlane."

"What does it open?"

"Nothing that I know of."

"Did you open Mr. Price's storage cupboard with it?"

"No, sir."

"All right." Chad handed the key back to Ethan.

"Are you going to believe that kid off the streets without no proof? Ain't you going to question him none about where my money is? How do you know what kind of crime he's been into? Don't know how you can rest easy in your beds with them orphans here."

Oscar Price was becoming more upset and angry by the moment.

Chad looked him in the eye and spoke calmly. "Oscar, if my boy says he didn't do it, I believe him. He didn't do it. Now I have to get back to my chores. Back to work, Ethan."

Ethan scurried off and Chad turned away, leaving a

sputtering Mr. Price to find his way out of the barn.

Luke was elated when he reported the incident to Henry and Polly at supper time.

"You should have seen it! Chad stood up for Ethan and sent old Price about his business. If you ask me, that man better keep an eye on his own boy."

"Just when did he think Ethan would be in town hanging around his general store, I want to know?" Polly was indignant. "I'd take an orphan like ours any day to some of the riffraff that runs around Willow Creek—including the Price boy."

Chad said nothing to the family about the visitor, and Ethan was grateful. When he went to bed that night, he thought about what the angry Mr. Price had said. What if Chad had believed what the man told him?

But he hadn't. Chad had called Ethan "my boy" and trusted his word. For the first time since they had arrived at the farm, Ethan went to sleep feeling that he truly belonged.

7

THE EXODUS

Ethan was reluctant to return to school after Christmas, but Manda was firm.

"You'll be without schooling, except for what we can give you, for a year or more. You need to finish out at least half your grade. Are you worried about what the other children are going to say?"

Ethan nodded. "Hector will tell them all just what he told his pa, and they'll believe him."

"The important thing is that we know it isn't true," Manda said. "You're a big boy, and you know how to pray. Just keep asking the Lord for strength to face them and trust in yourself. You'll get along fine."

Manda had followed through on her determination to confront Chad about their spiritual life when he returned from South Dakota. One morning, after the usual Bible reading and short prayer, Chad rose to go out to the fields.

"Chad, I need to talk to you."

Chad looked surprised, but sat down again. "Is it about getting ready for the trip? Things are coming along very well. As soon as you decide what must go, I'll have Henry or Luke—"

"No. It's about us. And the children."

"I thought we'd settled that. They'll do fine with Frances helping with their books. You'll have Polly to give a hand with the young ones on the trip, and we have a good place staked out."

Manda shook her head. "I'm not worried about that. It's our spiritual welfare that concerns me."

Chad looked blank. "What in the world has that got to do with anything?"

"Everything, I think. When Simon went with you, and we spent all that time worrying about him, I realized that I didn't really know how to trust the Lord. We've never talked much about our faith, Chad. We're both Christians, but it seems like just helping out at church and reading a few verses in the Bible isn't enough to give us the wisdom we need to raise these children."

"I think you're doing a good job, Manda. You make a fine mother. What are you having trouble with?"

"I need more patience," Manda replied. "A house with five children can't be perfect, and I like my house perfect. And I don't know how to show the children that I love them." She glanced at Chad. "I've never been much good at showing love."

"Might be partly 'cause I'm not really easy to get on

with," Chad admitted. "I guess I'm a pretty hard man when it come to young ones, but I want my children to respect me whether they like me or not." Chad ruffled his hair. "I suppose you're right. What do you think we should do?"

"Pray together," Manda replied promptly. "And talk things out. We need to teach the children to pray too. They won't learn unless they have a good example."

Having agreed to think it over, Chad departed for the field, and Manda made her way to the kitchen to work with Polly.

"How much storage room you reckon we'll have for canned goods?" Polly surveyed the rows of meat and vegetables and fruit that waited to be transferred to the cellar.

"We'll have to take it all, even if the men have to dig another root cellar. We may get an early garden in, but we can't depend on it. We've no idea what that land will grow. I've never heard that cottonwood trees gave off much fruit. Polly, did you ever teach a Sunday school class?"

Polly's mouth dropped open. "Sunday school? I thought we was talking about root cellars and fruit trees!"

"We were. But I've been thinking about the children. I'm sure we'll not be near enough to a church to attend regularly, and they need Bible training. It will be up to us to have our own services."

Polly regarded Manda thoughtfully. "Yep, I was right. You are different since them children came. Can't say as we couldn't all use a little sprucin' up in the disposition department. Everyone but Henry, maybe." She turned back to her work. "I suppose I could tell a few Bible stories and maybe learn some verses with them. That what you had in mind?"

"Yes. They need to know the Scriptures. Frances can teach them songs, and Henry will pray with them. We won't need a preacher."

"We got lots of preachers," Polly declared. "Talking to 'em on Sunday morning won't do as much as living packed into that soddy the rest of the week will show 'em. They'll get the picture."

Bert had returned to school, and Ethan confided in him on their first day back.

"I didn't mean for anyone to see the key. It fell out of my pocket by accident. Do you think it could open the storage cupboard at the store?"

"If Mr. Price said it did, I suppose it could. The important thing is that you didn't do it."

"That's what Manda said." Ethan sighed. "The only good thing about this is that both my folks believe me. I wish I could find out who really took the money."

"I could guess, but I won't," Bert replied. "Kids don't get away with stuff for very long. We'll find out sooner or later."

When the children returned from school, Ethan went directly to the barn. From the window Manda observed that he walked without his usual enthusiasm.

"Did the boys bother Ethan today?" she asked Frances.

"No. Mrs. Finch wouldn't allow it. She told the school that no one is guilty of anything just because someone says so. There has to be positive proof. Even if someone is proven wrong, Mrs. Finch says we have to ask ourselves three questions before we talk about it. Is it true? Is it kind? Is it necessary? She doesn't like telling tales or talking about other people."

Supper was a quiet meal, and Ethan didn't eat much. Even though no one at school had taunted him about Hector's story, he felt that the others were watching him and wondering if it were true.

Supper was not over when a knock came on the front door. This was not the usual time for callers, and the family waited in silence as Polly hurried to answer. Her voice came back to the dining room.

"Yes, sir, they're in. Wait here in the parlor, and I'll call 'em." She appeared in the doorway. "It's Oscar Price with Hector. He wants to see Chad and Ethan."

Ethan sank down in his seat and wished that he hadn't eaten any supper at all. He felt ill, and even the hard cold key in his pocket didn't offer much comfort. It was hard to pray when things were closing in on a person. Chad rose from the table and beckoned Ethan to follow him. Together they went into the parlor, and the door closed behind them.

"Evening, Oscar, Hector. Won't you sit down?"

"No, this won't take long." Oscar took his son by the shoulder and pushed him forward. "Go ahead, boy."

Hector swallowed nervously, and when he spoke his voice squeaked. "I come to tell you that it wasn't Ethan who opened Pa's cupboard. It was me. And I never used Ethan's key—it don't fit nothing. I used Pa's key. I said it was Ethan 'cause I didn't want the fellows to like no orphan better than me." Hector looked down at the floor. "I'm sorry," he muttered.

"Speak up, boy."

"I'm sorry, Mr. Rush. I'm sorry, Ethan."

Mr. Price turned toward the door and would have left without another word if Chad had not spoken.

"Thank you for coming. We'll consider this behind us. Oscar, it isn't enough just to go to church on Sunday. You and your boy need to pray together."

Oscar blinked in surprise. He'd never heard Chad Rush make a statement like that. Chad wasn't one to talk religion with his neighbors.

Oscar nodded. " 'Spect you're right. Come on, Hector. We'll be going."

Ethan felt as though a load had been lifted from his back, and suddenly he was hungry.

"Oscar Price found out who took his money," Chad announced when they returned to the table. "They came to tell us about it."

Ethan was grateful that nothing more was said, then or later. His last weeks at school in Willow Creek would be happy ones.

The days of preparation for the trip went by quickly—too quickly, according to Manda and Polly, who were faced with decisions about which household goods would be taken.

"I feel like a missionary, packing barrels for a foreign land," Polly grumbled. "If we knew what kind of town they had around there, we'd know what we don't need to take."

"Frances will pack hers and the children's clothes," Manda said. "I'll take care of the bedding and linens, and you see to the dishes and food. The men will crate the furniture to ship. We'll soon see what the town is like, because that's where the train will leave us."

"Luke says they're moving the livestock out to the depot today. How many freight cars did Chad hire?"

"Two, one for the animals and one for the household goods. He and Luke will go with the load, then Henry will leave with the wagon. Ethan is going with Henry."

"That leaves us and Frances and three young 'uns to take the passenger train. Sure hope there's someone to meet us." In spite of her grumbling, Polly was getting excited about the move. She had never been outside the state of Nebraska, and South Dakota seemed like a long way from home.

Everyone gathered in the yard to watch the animals being led toward town. The horses would be kept in the smithy's stable overnight, and the cows and pigs would be under the watchful eye of the farmer nearest the depot. Manda had other plans for her chickens and ducks.

"They'll go in the wagon with Henry. I'm not going to lose my flocks from having them scared to death by the dreadful racket of that freight car. I want them properly fed and watered."

"That's why Luke and I are going with the animals,

Manda," Chad told her, "but we'll be just as happy not to hear that cackling for several days."

The wagon would carry the bedding, extra clothing, and fresh food. It would also carry the organ. The discussion about the necessity of hauling that piece of furniture had been long and sometimes heated.

"There's no room in that soddy for anything we can't sit, sleep, or eat on. The organ doesn't qualify," Chad declared.

"Papa, I can't live without my organ."

"I'd call that an exaggeration. You can live without a lot of things."

"My spirit won't live."

"You're being dramatic, Frances. We won't talk about it any longer."

A few days later Frances broached the subject again.

"If the organ can't go, I'll stay here with Uncle George and Aunt Myra."

"That instrument is more important to you than your family?"

"No, but I wouldn't leave any of my family here either, just because they'd take up too much room. Please, Papa. We'll need it to have our own church services. It can go with Henry in the wagon."

So the organ was crated and ready to go, much to the relief of Frances and the children.

Simon was especially delighted. "I'm going to learn to play it when we get there. Frances said I could."

Frances hugged the little boy and assured him that they

would begin as soon as possible.

Alice was content to be going with Frances, but she did remember Lolly, the rag doll Ma had made for her. Manda had sewed a new outfit for the doll and tucked scraps of material in around dishes and other boxes for later use in sewing instruction.

Will treasured his cherry stick horse with the leather straps and wouldn't hear of its being packed or carried in the wagon.

"My horse goes on the train. It always goes on the train," he said.

"He may as well enjoy his horse," Manda said to Polly "I'm certainly going to miss mine."

Chad had decided that they wouldn't take the small buggy or the horse that drew it.

"That would be a long trip for the buggy and the horse. Out there on the prairie there won't be such a thing as a short visit to the neighbors. If we need to go to town for supplies, the wagon will be more practical. Besides, we have no extra driver for the buggy."

Manda agreed that this was so, but she knew that it would be hard not to be able to venture out when she chose.

As the day approached for them to leave, everyone was more quiet than usual. Manda looked wistfully at her flower beds and lamented that she would not see them bloom. Frances mourned the loss of her school friends, and Polly looked around her kitchen with new appreciation.

"Never done my cooking in the living room before. And it's been a long time since I had to do washing outside. What other good things will be waiting for us out there in the wild?"

"Indians!" Simon told her. "And animals like we never see around here."

"I can't wait," Polly said.

Only the men had no time to ponder what they were leaving behind. All their effort and thought were required to arrange for the shipping and to get everything into town at the right time. It was two days before all the furniture and household goods were packed into the freight car.

To Ethan's great pleasure, he was allowed to spend the last two days with Bert. Hannah and Carl made him feel at home, and he was soon convinced that living in a soddy would be the best of all worlds.

Frances stayed with a friend in town, and Polly solved the problem of the three youngest Coopers.

"I'll take 'em home with me. I need to get Ma settled in with the neighbor, and the children can run around our place just as well as they can here. Ma's been asking what them orphans look like—as if they wouldn't look like any other young 'uns she's ever seen."

Manda left with an easy mind to enjoy a final visit with Lydia Archer.

As impossible as it may have seemed, everything fell into place. The freight cars with Chad and Luke left on time. Henry, Ethan, and the wagon pulled away from the house in the early morning dark, waved off by George and

Myra. The passenger train became the temporary home for
the rest of the family. The exodus of the Rush household
was under way.

8

ON THE
TRAIN AGAIN

The train carrying the family toward their new life on the prairie wasn't crowded when Manda, Polly, and the children boarded. It had left Sioux City three days ago, but most of the passengers had no desire to travel into the northern wilderness of Nebraska and had long since departed.

The car into which Manda and Polly settled the children had only three other travelers. One, an elderly man, slept soundly in his seat. His mustache lifted and fell with his breathing, and his head rolled dangerously against the back of his seat. Polly regarded him with alarm.

"His neck is going to snap and his head'll roll afore we reach the next town," she declared. "Someone ought to wake him up."

"I'll do it!" Simon volunteered.

"No, you won't," Manda told him. "He hasn't lost his

head yet, so chances are he won't. He is going to have one sore neck, though."

"I'm going to watch, just in case it does come off," Simon declared. "I've never seen that happen before."

A second man sat near the front of the car, his attention centered on the book in his hand. The noise of the wheels and the swaying of the coach didn't distract him. Frances observed that he was young, tall (judging by the long leg that stretched out into the aisle), handsome, and nicely dressed. While the others were settling into their seats, Frances improved her time by speculating as to where he was going, what he did for a living, and why he was alone. He was not, she decided, a farmer or a teacher. At least he didn't look like any farmer or teacher she had ever seen.

The third traveler was most interesting to Will. The little boy's eyes remained riveted upon her while Polly lifted him into the seat and placed a book in his lap.

"Alice," he asked, "is this the circus train?"

"No. This is a family train. Where do you see any animals?"

"No animals," Will replied. "But there's a circus lady."

Alice looked in the direction Will pointed. He could well be right, she thought. The woman sitting ahead of them in the car was certainly unlike anyone they had seen in Willow Creek. It was not her uncommon size that had attracted Will's attention, although she did require the whole seat for herself. It was the huge hat that adorned her head. Shaped like a flat basket, this unusual headgear contained an amazing variety of objects.

Fruit of every description, mingled with brightly colored flowers, was most prominent. In the midst of this perched a large white bird with wings outspread. Stretched over the whole scene was a veil, tied securely under an ample chin. As an added precaution against the possibility of tipping over, the hat was secured by long pins with knobs on the end. These knobs, Will noted, were carved in the shape of faces. He stared in fascination.

"Will, it's not polite to stare," Alice told him.

"What is that on her head?"

"It's a hat. Now quit staring."

Will glanced at the small straw head covering that Polly wore. Now that was a hat, he thought. Even the slightly fancier one that Manda had removed and placed on the seat beside her qualified for the name, in his opinion. But not the one the lady wore. Will knew that as long as anyone was watching, he dare not slide from his seat and get a closer look. He would wait for the appropriate moment.

"Mama," Frances said after a time, "could we go to the dining car and get some lemonade?"

Manda opened her eyes wearily. "You'll have to get it, Frances. I'm worn to a frazzle. Take some money from my bag." She closed her eyes again.

"I want to go too," Simon said. "I can help you carry it back."

"Does anyone else want to come?" Frances waited a moment, but Alice was curled in a corner with a book, and Will recognized his opportunity. He shook his head.

As soon as Frances and Simon disappeared into the car ahead, Will looked carefully at Polly and Manda. They were both asleep. Quietly the little boy slid to the floor and picked up his stick horse. In case anyone awoke, he would have an excuse for being in the aisle. Covered by the noise of the train, he disturbed no one on his journey toward the empty seat behind The Hat.

It took only a moment to climb up and lean over the back of the lady's seat. His stick still in his hand, Will braced himself and gazed at the peculiar sight. He looked carefully to be sure that the woman was asleep, then cautiously he raised his finger to trace the lines of the face on the hat pin knob.

At that moment Alice looked up and saw him. "Will! What are you doing? Get down from there!"

Startled, the little boy turned quickly toward his sister. The stick horse was forgotten, and it connected sharply with the big hat. The pins were not sufficient to hold it, and the basket of fruit and flowers slid down over the woman's eyes and nose. It did not cover her mouth, however, and the screech that emerged brought the whole car to life instantly.

The young man dropped his book and sprang to his feet. The older gentleman jerked upright and shouted, "What? What? What?"

Polly was the first to act, and she hurried up the aisle to help the poor distressed lady. Manda looked frantically about for Will.

"He fell off the seat," Alice informed her.

Manda found him face down on the floor between the seats, sobbing wildly, badly frightened over the uproar he had caused.

Polly returned, shaking her head. "She thought her sight was gone. Small wonder, with a peck of fruit down over her face. That hat must weigh five pounds at least. Never saw such a spectacle in my life. She's going to be all of a tremble for the rest of the trip."

Manda sighed. "We haven't been on the train for two hours yet, and we have two days to go. I hope we all survive."

She rose and took Will by the hand. "We need to go and apologize to the lady. You can leave your horse here this time."

"She ain't got no idea what hit her," Polly said. "Maybe you better leave well enough alone."

"I have an idea what hit her," Manda replied. "Will needs to learn that he can't do something like that without taking responsibility for it." She marched a reluctant Will ahead of her to the seat where the woman sat, fanning herself with a magazine.

"I'm Manda Rush. My son has something he would like to say to you. Go ahead, Will."

"Will, is it? My name is Eunice Martin." The lady smiled at him, and Will burst into tears again.

"I didn't mean to hit you with my horse. I wanted to see the faces."

Mrs. Martin appeared confused. "I know I have more than one chin, but I have only one face. And you say you hit me with a horse?" She looked to Manda for an explanation, and Manda told her what had happened.

Eunice Martin laughed heartily. "Now don't worry, young man. There was no harm done. We can all get acquainted now." She looked around the coach, and the two men stood up.

"Major John Emory, at your service, ma'am."

"And I'm Timothy Flynn." The younger man shook hands with Mrs. Martin and Manda.

When Frances and Simon returned with the lemonade, they found the entire group gathered in the middle of the car, visiting like old friends.

"This is my daughter Frances, and my son Simon," Manda told them.

Frances felt her face grow warm as the young man rose and offered her a seat beside him. All of them, it appeared, were going to the same place, but at Winner they would go their separate ways.

That night, as the train rattled through the darkness, no one was awake to see the freight cars they passed or to wonder why they stood silently on the siding.

The cars that Chad and Luke had packed with animals, farm implements, and furniture had left Willow Creek in good time. Since their progress was slower than the passenger train, they had departed the day before the family set out. There seemed to be an unusual number of delays. New freight was taken on at various points along the way, and engines were switched.

"Good thing we brought plenty of food and water for

the animals," Luke remarked.

"Yes, we may not always stop in a place as convenient as this."

Chad watched the cows as they grazed along the tracks. A stream flowed nearby, the horse basked in the early spring sun. They had several hours to wait before their cars would be picked up again.

"Sam told us that we wouldn't go straight through," Chad said. "He thought we'd get there by the time Manda and the family did, though. At the rate we're moving right now, they'll be waiting for us."

"Guess I could go rustle us some dinner. Might's well get it out of the way before we load the animals again."

Luke headed for the car that held the household goods. Considering the number of pieces of furniture and other items packed in, it was remarkably homelike. The men's bedrolls had been placed near the big sliding door, and a cupboard holding food and dishes stood conveniently near. Luke grinned to himself as he remembered their first day out.

The two men had sat in the doorway of the freight car as it swayed and bumped over the rails. They were both tired after having spent two days getting everything loaded. One cow had been particularly ornery and refused to walk up the ramp. It had taken four of them to get her settled in the makeshift stall, and now, half a day into the trip, they could hear her bawling her displeasure.

"She's going to have one sore throat if she keeps that

up," Luke remarked. "And I'm going to have a headache."

"My head is the only thing that isn't sore," Chad said. "I've used muscles I didn't know I had lifting that furniture. It was good of Sam and Swartz to lend a hand."

"Do you think we'll get it all in that soddy?"

Chad nodded. "I think so. There won't be room to dance around the middle of the floor, but with the beds along the wall for the children and the bunkhouse for you and Henry and Ethan, we'll manage. Everyone will spend most of their time outdoors."

The men talked about the task that lay ahead of them.

"We'll need to get Polly's garden plowed first off," Luke said. "She'll walk back to Willow Creek if she doesn't have a decent garden."

"I'm counting on the Indians to help get the house up before winter. We can work on the inside when the weather's bad."

"Good thing you cleared for planting last fall. Henry and I can get the wheat and corn in before the end of the month."

"Ethan's turned out to be good help," Chad said. "He's going to be a successful farmer one day. Simon's getting big enough to help too."

"There'll be plenty of work to go around," Luke predicted. "This first year won't be easy. Well, guess it's time to milk and feed the stock."

He jumped down and trotted back to the car behind them. Chad followed and swung himself up on the ladder and into the car.

"I wonder where Manda put the liniment," he said. "I sure need something for my aches, or I'll never move in the morning."

"I could use some, too," Luke admitted. "But we'll have to leave the door open all night, or the fumes will take us out. We won't live to see morning."

"I'll risk it." Chad finished putting food in the stalls, and they returned to the front car.

"When do we move again?"

Chad consulted the schedule Sam had given him. "Two a.m. And we don't stop again until tomorrow evening. We'll make good time tomorrow. How about some food before we hunt that liniment?"

The men turned to survey the stacked-up furniture and discovered a fatal flaw in their packing.

"Where's the cupboard?" Chad asked.

"You mean the one with all the food in it?" Luke scratched his chin. "I'd say it's somewhere behind all that other stuff. I seem to recollect that we loaded it first."

"That means we don't eat until we move all this furniture."

"Yep. Something like that. How long do you reckon a body can go without food? There's nothing left of what Polly packed for us this morning, is there?"

A search around the open space revealed that there wasn't.

An hour later, the men had dragged the cupboard to the front and pushed the rest of the goods back into place.

"Now I'm too tired to eat," Luke huffed as he wiped his

face on a red bandanna. "That was one knob-headed thing to do. What's in there that doesn't have to be chewed?"

A day later, as Luke pulled food from the cupboard and prepared to light a fire to cook dinner, he looked off toward the north and thought of their destination. They would be a little late, but Henry and Ethan would get to Winner in time to meet the family. Chad had arranged to hire a dray to have their goods moved to the homestead. The end of the journey was in sight.

By the third day on the train, Manda and Polly were ready for the news that they would reach Winner by morning. Only Frances wasn't anxious to have the trip end. She was already feeling sad about parting from Timothy, whose company she had enjoyed as often as her mother allowed. The younger children had been entertained by the Major and Mrs. Martin, both of whom knew stories that kept them spellbound.

"If they went according to schedule, the freight cars should be there when we arrive," Manda said. "And Chad figured that Henry would make it before we do too. I'll certainly be glad to have everyone back together again. Is everything ready to take off the train?"

Polly assured her that it was. "It's only the Lord's good mercy that we been able to keep track of Frances and the young 'uns without more disaster than we had. I almost envy them men with nothing more than animals and a wagon to look after. It's always the women as takes the brunt of moving a household."

Shortly before daybreak the train pulled into the small town of Winner. The children scrambled down and raced across the platform. Frances, Manda, and Polly stepped out and looked around expectantly. There was no one in sight.

ETHAN IN CHARGE

Ethan turned in the wagon seat and looked back at the big house they were leaving. Even though it was not yet daylight, he could see the dim outline through the trees. It seemed as though he could still see George and Myra waving to them.

Henry glanced over at the boy. "Homesick already? We won't even be off Chad's land for another hour or so."

"Not homesick, exactly. I was kind of worried about how George would take care of everything without us. There's a lot of work to do here."

"George knows how to handle it. You need to be thinking of all the work you'll have to do on the new place. Won't be easy, breaking ground and putting up a house. Things won't be like they've been here."

"I know. But I don't mind the work. And living in a soddy will be great. Bert sure likes it."

"Manda and Polly aren't all that anxious to try it out."
Henry laughed. "Polly likes things convenient, and Manda
likes them comfortable. They're not likely to have either
one out there. Not for a while, anyway."

Ethan was quiet for so long that Henry thought he
might have gone to sleep. Suddenly he spoke again.

"Henry, what about the Indians?"

"What about them?"

"Are they dangerous?"

"The ones we saw were friendly. I expect there are still
some up there who don't care much for white folks."

"Why not?"

"Well . . ." Henry struggled to find a way to explain to
the boy what was largely a mystery to him. "Not too many
years ago, all the land where we're going belonged to the
Indians. They had their way of life and got along fine. Then
the government took some of the land to run a railway to
the west."

"They just took it?"

Henry shrugged. "I guess they might have paid a little
something for it, but they pushed the Indians into just a few
sections called reservations, and a lot of the land went to
white ranchers."

"Like us?"

"Mmm, something like that. Only Chad bought the land
fair and square from the government. He didn't buy any
reservation land. Anyway, pretty soon the Indians couldn't
run their cattle on the open range any longer, because the
ranchers put up barbed wire fences around their land."

"That doesn't sound fair."

"Nope. 'Tweren't fair. That's why some of the Indians still ain't sure about white folks. They feel they've been cheated. It would be something like a bunch of people pushing Chad onto his back forty and not giving him full price for the rest of it." Henry thought for a moment. "Then again, mebbe not. No one ever got the best of Chad Rush in a deal. And Chad's a fair man. He won't take advantage of the Indians or anyone else."

Ethan silently hoped the Indians knew that. Living across the river from a whole reservation of them might be scary.

The sun came up, surrounded by dark red clouds. "Storm coming," Henry predicted. "Good thing we have our load covered. We can sleep in the wagon tonight if we need to."

Ethan looked at the sky. "How do you know it's going to storm? It looks pretty bright to me."

"Red sky in the morning, sailors take warning. Red sky at night, sailors delight," Henry quoted. "Besides, this is the time of year for storms."

Ethan sifted in his seat. "We don't seem to be getting very far. I could walk as fast as this."

"Go ahead," Henry told him. "Do you good to run some. If you haven't noticed, this isn't the best road in the United States. It's had a long, hard winter."

Ethan jumped down from the wagon and ran on ahead. The air was cool and fresh, and the wind blowing through his hair felt good. He was glad Chad had thought he was responsible enough to go along with Henry.

The sun was high when they stopped beside a small stream to eat the dinner Polly had prepared.

"It makes you hungry to travel, doesn't it?" Ethan chewed happily on a ham sandwich. "What are we having tonight?"

"You haven't even finished this meal, and you're thinking about the next one?" Henry laughed at him and ruffled his hair. "I don't blame you. That Polly is a mighty good cook. I think we have some stew to warm up."

While Henry dozed with his hat over his face, Ethan explored the creek and surrounding field. A rabbit bounded past, and small bugs rose from the tall grass. Ethan returned to the wagon when he tired of waving them away from his face and bare arms.

"They swarm all over you when there's rain coming," Henry said when Ethan complained. "Never could understand why Noah didn't swat some of these pests when he only had two of 'em."

"God didn't tell him to," Ethan said. "So they must be good for something."

"Guess we'd better get moving." Henry got up and checked the harness. "Have a ways to go yet before evening. Don't supposed you'd like to drive awhile, would you?"

Ethan beamed. "Sure. Be glad to." He climbed up on the seat and picked up the heavy reins. "Giddap." He slapped the leather down.

The horses stood, swishing their tails.

Henry chuckled. "You got to lay them down harder than that. They think there's flies on their back."

After a few more tries, the big horses moved forward. Ned flicked his ears and tossed his head, causing Ethan to fear that he might run away.

"Nope," Henry reassured him. "For one thing, Jesse won't let him. For another, he doesn't want to work that hard."

Ethan was more than pleased with his new responsibility, even though he soon realized that the horses needed no direction.

"Wait 'til I tell Simon and Alice what I did. They won't believe that I can handle horses by myself."

"You'll handle more than horses by yourself before the year's over," Henry predicted. "Nothing like living on a prairie to turn you into a man."

Ethan pondered this as they rode along. He had no knowledge of what it meant to homestead a new area, but he was anxious to find out. The year ahead looked like a big adventure to him.

They stopped before dark. After rubbing down the horses and turning them loose to graze, Henry turned his attention to setting up for the night.

"Gather some pieces of wood, Ethan, and I'll give you a lesson in building a good fire." Henry instructed the boy how to make a circle of rocks and mound the dirt in the center. They placed some kindling and twigs around it, then added some chunks of wood that Henry had brought from home. They soon had a bright fire burning and a kettle of Polly's stew warming on it.

"I never had a better supper than this," Ethan declared as they ate.

"Everything tastes better over an open fire," Henry said. "Tomorrow night we'll put some potatoes in the coals to roast. You'll see how good those can be."

They were on the way early in the morning. It had rained hard during the night, though Ethan hadn't heard it. Now, however, the grass glistened and the trees dripped. The day was fine, and promised to be good weather for traveling.

"How much farther do we have to go?"

"We should be close to the state border by tomorrow night," Henry told him. "Then it will be another full day to Winner. Takes longer than the train, but I'd rather go this way."

"Me, too. I lived on a train long enough. Not that it wasn't fun," Ethan hastened to add, "but I've lived in a house for a year now, and I like it better."

As they traveled, Henry pointed out an occasional deer loping across the prairie. Once he spotted a buffalo off in the distance.

"Will it come this way?"

"Not likely. They keep pretty much to themselves."

"It looks a lot like a cow, only bigger."

"They're related to the oxen," Henry said. "Some ranchers out here plow with them."

Ethan nodded. "I remember Mr. Glover telling us that. We won't need to as long as we have Ned and Jesse, will we?"

"Probably not. But buffalo graze on our land, and the Indians use them for food and skins."

The next day's progress was slower. Not only was the trail rougher and harder to follow, but Henry was forced to stop several times to make small repairs to the wagon. Finally, just before noon, they came upon a stream, and nearby, a large shade tree.

"This looks like a good place to rest," Henry said. "We'll have some dinner, even if it is a little early." He jumped down from the high seat, and a moment later fell to the ground.

Ethan scrambled to look over at him.

"Stay there, Ethan!" Henry shouted, then a shot sounded close to Ethan's head.

"What's the matter, Henry?" Ethan screamed, then he watched the scene before him in horror.

Henry unlaced his boot, pulled up his pant leg, and grabbed a knife from his belt. Swiftly he cut a gash on the side of his leg, then tied a bandanna tightly above the wound.

"Henry! What are you doing?" Ethan was sobbing with fright.

"Now take it easy, boy. I stepped on a rattler, and he bit me. I can't get up and walk, or the poison will go through me. Can you get some water in the bucket?"

Ethan nodded, though he wasn't sure his legs would support him. The snake lay dead beside Henry, and Ethan tried to avoid looking at it as he dropped to the ground and grabbed the bucket from the side of the wagon. When he returned with the water, Henry's leg had already begun to swell.

He smiled weakly at Ethan. "Get a towel from the back."
Ethan hastened to do so.

"Now listen carefully. I need you to go and find some
snake root. It's a tall plant with spiky leaves and a bunch of
little white flowers on a stem. The flowers come to a point
at the top. Be sure you bring the whole plant." Henry was
breathing harder, and sweat was coming out on his
forehead. "Hurry, now."

Ethan turned and raced toward the field of weeds and
flowers at the side of the trail. He didn't want to leave
Henry alone, but he knew he must follow instructions.
Wildly he looked around, searching for the plant that
Henry had described.

Ethan dropped to his knees. Tears ran down his face as
he searched frantically among the weeds and wildflowers. If
only he knew what he was looking for!

"You look for something?"

Startled, Ethan whipped around to find a tall sun-
browned man behind him. An Indian! How could he have
come out of nowhere so silently? Ethan crouched in the
grass and stared at the man in terror. Black hair hung in
one braid down the Indian's back. He wore soft buckskin
leggings and jacket. A large bow hung over his shoulder,
but he also carried a rifle on one arm. Was he friendly?

The Indian spoke again. "You alone?"

Ethan shook his head and began to cry again. He turned
and pointed toward the wagon.

"Henry. He got bit by a rattlesnake, and I can't find the
right medicine."

The Indian turned, and Ethan saw the horse that had been behind the big man. A girl about his own age regarded him solemnly from the horse's back. She also had black braided hair, and she wore a soft buckskin dress with fringe on the sleeves and hem. Her legs were bare, but on her feet were moccasins, decorated with brightly colored beads.

"Gray Dawn, you bring snake root," said the man, lifting her down from the horse. Then he mounted and rode off in the direction Ethan had pointed.

Ethan jumped to his feet, embarrassed that the girl had seen him cry. Quickly he scrubbed his fists across his face, leaving streaks of dirt from his forehead to his chin.

The girl said nothing, and Ethan glanced anxiously toward the wagon. Would the Indian kill Henry—maybe scalp him? What would happen to Ethan?

"Red Cloud will help." The girl's soft voice caused Ethan to look up.

"Is he your father?"

The girl nodded. Taking Ethan's hand in hers, she plunged deeper into the tall grass. Ethan was surprised to see that she was as tall as he, and while she moved easily over the uneven ground, Ethan stumbled and had trouble keeping up with her. She soon found what she was looking for and dropped down beside it.

"Snake root."

Ethan reached to grab the plant, but she shook her head. "Not flower. Root."

Picking up a smooth, flat rock, Gray Dawn began to dig

deeply into the soil. Grabbing the heavy stem, she pulled
the plant out, shook the dirt from it, and handed it to
Ethan. Very soon they had two handfuls of snake root.

Henry was lying in the back of the wagon when the
children arrived. His eyes were closed, and Ethan's heart
dropped. "Please, please, Lord. Don't let Henry die. We
can't get along without Henry."

Ethan was so concerned that he forgot that anyone was
listening to him. The Indian was gently bathing Henry's
face with a towel dipped in cold water.

"Red Cloud knows what to do," Gray Dawn told him.
She handed Red Cloud the snake root plants.

"You bathe," he told her, and as Ethan watched, the
Indian ground the plant roots between two stones. Then,
mixing it with water, he began to put a small amount of the
liquid between Henry's lips. He continued to give him more
every so often, and by the end of the afternoon, Henry was
looking better. Still Red Cloud and Gray Dawn stayed by,
and Ethan was grateful.

As evening approached, Ethan felt that he should offer
his guests some food. Carefully he started a fire as Henry
had showed him and set the pot of stew on it to warm. The
corn bread and apple pie that Polly had sent with them
completed the meal, and his new friends seemed satisfied.
When darkness fell, they checked again on Henry. His
fever seemed to be gone, and he slept quietly.

"We stay," Red Cloud announced, and he unfastened
bedrolls for himself and Gray Dawn. Ethan unrolled his

beside them and lay down gratefully. He fell asleep instantly.

Before daylight, Ethan smelled smoke. Henry must be getting breakfast.

Henry! Ethan's eyes opened at once as he recalled what had happened. Red Cloud stood by the fire, and Gray Dawn knelt before a pan of food that smelled awfully good.

"Henry?"

"Better. You see." Red Cloud nodded toward the wagon, and Ethan ran over to it. Henry was lying with his head on the flour sack, and he grinned at Ethan.

"Hey, where's my breakfast, boy? You didn't give me any supper last night." Henry's voice was weak, but he spoke cheerfully.

"Henry, are you going to be all right? You're not going to die?"

"Not unless I die of starvation. Our friend looked after me all night. The Lord was with us, Ethan."

Ethan nodded. "I prayed awful hard. Manda told me I'd be all right if I asked the Lord for strength and trusted Him. He heard us pray."

Ethan brought his plate of food and sat beside Henry to eat. "Will we stay here until you get well?"

"I think we'd better move on. Chad and Manda will be terribly worried if we don't show up. They'll have to wait for us as it is, but I'd hate for them to come looking for us. I think Chad will give a day's leeway. You can handle the wagon just fine. I'll be right here to tell you what to do if you need help."

Ethan was proud and scared at the same time. If Henry trusted him, he would do his best to get them to Winner. By sunup, Red Cloud had hitched Ned and Jesse to the wagon and mounted his own horse. Gray Dawn, seated behind him, smiled timidly at Ethan and said good-bye.

"You do fine, young brave." Red Cloud lifted his hand in farewell and, turning, galloped off toward the west. Ethan watched them, wishing that the big Indian were riding along beside them, even for a little while.

Straightening his back, Ethan called back to Henry. "We're ready. You let me know if you want something."

Several times during that long day, Ethan thought he saw the big horse with the two riders out of the corner of his eye, but when he turned to look, there was nothing but tall prairie grass, blowing in the wind.

TOGETHER
AGAIN

Manda and Polly stood gazing up and down the railway track. The train from which they had just alighted had disappeared from sight. There were no freight cars on the siding, nor was there a heavily loaded wagon sitting beside the small station house. Manda wasn't ready to believe her eyes.

"They have to be here. They all left before we did. Chad figured the time and even allowed for delays. Where are they?"

"We know where they ain't." Polly grabbed Will as he raced by. "Don't you get out of sight now. We're already missing more folks than we can spare."

"Maybe they got here last night and went to the hotel," Frances suggested.

"And took the freight cars? I think we'd better check with the station master."

"Nope," was his reply to their inquiry. "Ain't been no freight left here this month. Ain't seen no wagon with two fellas on it, neither. You sure this is where they was supposed to come?"

"From what I saw coming through this wilderness, they didn't have a whole lot of choice," Polly told him. "There ain't no other town around, is there?"

"Nope."

"Lot of help he is," Polly sniffed as they went back out to the platform. "Looks to me like we got to solve our own problems."

"Beg pardon, ma'am." Major Emory approached Manda. "May I suggest that you and your family go to the hotel until the train arrives? Your wagon driver will be able to locate you if they should arrive later."

Manda agreed that this seemed a sensible plan, and they retired to the hotel. The following day they spent on the station platform, but no one appeared.

"There can't be two Winners in this world and us at the wrong one," Polly declared. "You'd think one or the other of the men would be here by now."

The next day Frances stayed at the hotel and entertained the children while Manda and Polly took up their post at the station. The morning train brought no extra freight cars, but the station master reported that the train due that afternoon had picked up two cars back thirty miles in Burke.

"I don't recall seeing any town thirty miles back," Polly said.

"Never said it was a town. Folks name the fence posts out here." The man trudged back into his station, leaving the two ladies to ponder the mysteries of prairie life.

Frances and the children appeared to announce that they were hungry.

"I suppose we might as well go back to the hotel for dinner," Manda said. "The train won't be here for several hours. My, I'll be glad to see us all together again."

"Look!" Simon shouted. "A wagon! I see our wagon!"

The family raced to the end of the platform to watch the small object in the distance. Polly shielded her eyes from the sun. "There's something on the trail, all right. Could be buffalo for all I can tell, but it's likely enough a wagon."

They waited impatiently for the object to come closer, chattering excitedly. As it drew nearer, and it was determined that it was indeed a wagon, they fell silent.

"It can't be ours," Frances said finally. "There's only one person in it."

In the time it took the wagon to cover the distance, many thoughts occurred to Manda. Ethan had gotten lost. Ethan had become ill and died. Henry had buried him on the prairie. They had been stopped by the Indians, and Ethan had been kidnapped.

"Oh," she moaned. "We never should have let the boy go with Henry. I should have kept him with me where I'd know he was safe. I wish I'd insisted—"

"Don't waste your wishes," Polly interrupted. "Ethan's driving the wagon. Start worrying about where Henry is, if you need something to keep you busy."

It was a great relief when they saw Henry emerge from the back of the wagon. He was pale and weak, and decidedly thinner than he had been when they all left home, but he assured them that he was fine. A day's rest, he said, and he'd be back to himself.

"You can thank Ethan for getting us here. We wouldn't have made it without him."

Ethan beamed happily at the praise, and after a hug from everyone, he and Henry told the astonished family the story of their trip. The younger ones insisted that he tell them again about the Indian and his daughter, Gray Dawn.

"Were you scared, Ethan?"

"I was at first. I didn't even hear him coming. All of a sudden, there he was. But when he helped Henry get better, I wasn't afraid anymore. He ate Polly's stew and corn bread and said it was good."

"Well, I should hope so," Polly said, but she looked pleased. "I'll fix them some more if they come to visit us."

"Now if only Chad and Luke would get here, I'd feel easy in my mind." Manda looked anxiously down the track.

In the late afternoon the train appeared and, to everyone's relief, the freight cars with the two men and the rest of the goods were attached to it. The cars were put on a siding to await the transfer to a dray.

Chad was surprised to hear that Henry and Ethan had arrived only hours ahead of them, and their story had to be repeated.

"I'm proud of you, boy," Chad said to Ethan when they

had finished. "You can work right alongside the men on this homestead. You've proven that you can handle hard times."

Ethan felt as though he had grown a foot and aged a year since they had left Willow Creek. He wished Bert were there to share his happiness with him.

"Now we'd like to know where you two have been," Manda said. "How could it possibly take four days, even for a freight train?"

"Well, if we'd come straight north the way we were supposed to, it wouldn't have," Luke said.

"What do you mean?" Polly demanded. "North is the only way you could go."

"That shows how much you know about it," Luke retorted, and proceeded to tell what had happened. . . .

The second morning of their journey was cool and clear, and again Chad and Luke sat in the open door of their freight car and looked out over the prairie.

"Scenery sure doesn't change much, does it?" Luke chewed on a piece of straw and squinted at the sky. "Nice day for something besides setting on a railroad track."

Chad agreed. "I'm getting lazy, not doing anything but feeding and milking." He looked at his watch. "We aren't due to leave here until midmorning. What say we hunt a few rabbits for our dinner?"

The men grabbed their rifles, jumped down from the car, and waded into the tall grass directly in front of them. They scanned the territory carefully.

"We're almost at the state border, aren't we?"

Chad nodded. "Another day and half should do it. I wonder how Henry is doing with the wagon. I'm glad he took Ethan with him. The boy will be company, even if he can't do much."

They walked on in silence. Birds flew up and insects swarmed around them, but the hunters failed to scare out any rabbits.

Suddenly Luke stopped and turned his head sharply.

"Did you hear that? Sounds like a train."

Chad pulled his watch out again. "Can't be. It isn't time for the morning passenger, and there's no freight due."

It was soon evident that it was a train, due or not. The men turned and ran back toward the track. It wasn't easy going. Luke tripped in a gopher hole and dropped his gun, and by that time the train had stopped.

"They're taking our cars on!" Luke shouted. "Stop! Wait for us!"

He couldn't be heard, and no one glanced in their direction. By the time the men reached the rails, the cars were beginning to move slowly away. With one last desperate sprint, they caught the bars at the back of the freight car and pulled themselves up.

"That was close," Luke panted. "They almost got away without us."

Chad puffed in silence for a moment, trying to regain his breath. "I'd sure like it better if we were going the right way," he said finally. "This train is headed south. . . ."

"It was true," Luke concluded. "The southbound freight

had picked us up, and we went a hundred miles back the way we came. All the freight master would say was that we should have waited till we got to where we were going before we went hunting."

"All I can say is I hope if we ever get to that homestead we can stay put," Polly declared. "Couldn't nothing worse happen than we've already had traveling to it."

The following morning everyone turned out to watch the transfer of the furniture from the freight car to the dray that Chad hired. The dray was a vehicle that the children were not familiar with, and they watched closely as it was loaded.

"That wagon only has two wheels," Simon commented. "And it's awful close to the ground. Will it really hold all of the furniture?"

"Yes, it will," Luke assured him. "It's built to carry heavy loads and to be hauled by one ox. Everything will get there fine. You'll see."

Manda's heart dropped as she looked at "everything" that was packed onto the dray. How would she manage with so little furniture? Only the most essential items had been moved. The large kitchen table, chairs, cupboard, and small cook stove were loaded on. Manda's sewing machine was strapped on top. She had wanted to bring the parlor sofa, but Chad said there would not be room for it.

"As soon as the house is built, we'll have George ship the rest of the things," he had promised. "We'll have to make do with beds built against the walls until then."

The last leg of the trip was uneventful, but it was a weary group of travelers who finally came in sight of the cottonwood trees and the river flowing behind them. There wasn't much daylight left, and they were all content to eat a cold supper and roll out their blankets wherever they found room.

In the early morning dawn, Manda looked out the door of the soddy.

"Things always look better by daylight," she said.

"They couldn't look any worse," Polly grumbled. She gazed around the large space that would be their home. "How am I going to keep this place clean?"

"You don't have to scrub the floor or wash the windows," Alice told her. "And you get to wash clothes outdoors!"

"Lucky me," Polly said. "I can get breakfast out there too."

The furniture was soon unloaded and moved in, and Manda set about making the soddy as homelike as possible. Everyone had a hand in moving canned food into the root cellar, and by the end of the second day, the prairie home was in running order.

Chad's first concern was to replenish his livestock. Sheep and cattle were soon grazing on his land, and Luke and Henry planted fields of wheat and corn. Under the watchful eye of Polly, Ethan was given the task of plowing her garden. Alice learned how to carefully wash and shine the lamp globes until they glistened. Simon fed the pigs and chickens, and gathered the eggs. There was more than enough work for everyone.

One hardship for Manda was the fact that there could be no word from Willow Creek unless one of the men had an errand in Winner.

"I feel as though I've left the world," she told Polly. "I didn't know what it would be like not to be able to run into town whenever I need something."

"Speaking of needing something, we're coming to the end of the soap we brought with us. Somebody will have to get to town pretty soon, or we're in trouble."

Chad was approached with the problem that evening. "I'll have Silver Wing come this week. She'll help you."

"The Indians sell soap?" Polly was skeptical.

"No, she'll help you make it."

"That's not what I had in mind," Polly told him. "I didn't know anyone made soap these days. This is the twentieth century."

"The rest of the country may be in the twentieth century, but we aren't," Manda said. "We're starting history over again. When are you going to butcher, Chad?"

"Tomorrow. I'll have Henry make a soap frame, and Ethan can get ashes out there. Thursday should be a good day for soap making."

"My, he's a great encouragement," Polly said when Chad left. "Provides all kinds of things to make our work harder."

At least three members of the family were pleased with the activity that week. They were not allowed near the area where the men were butchering, but Alice, Simon, and

Will watched the soap making with fascination.

Silver Wing arrived early from the reservation across the river. She was a good-natured woman with a cheerful smile creasing her brown face. The fact that she carried an equally cheerful papoose on her back didn't keep her from working hard.

A large iron kettle was placed over the fire, and Ethan was instructed to pour the ashes into it. Manda and Frances carried boiling water from the soddy, and Silver Wing stirred the mixture briskly with a long wooden paddle she had brought with her. Next she added the pig's fat, and the soap boiled and bubbled for the rest of the morning.

When it was pronounced ready, Simon was sent to get the men to pour the liquid into the frame.

"It should be ready to cut into bars by evening," Chad said. "We'll leave it here to cool."

Will wrinkled his nose. "It smells awful!"

"You didn't expect it would smell like cookies coming from the oven, did you?" Polly put her arm around him. "If it keeps you clean this summer, it will do its job. Come on now and help me in the garden."

Will dug around and pulled a few weeds, but soon he tired of that and wandered off toward the soddy.

Everyone had gone off to his own job, and the big room was empty. Since Polly had mentioned cookies, Will decided that he might as well have one or two. Dragging a chair to the cupboard, he climbed up to reach the cookie jar. At eye level with a shelf, he spied Polly's big bottle of vanilla. This was what made the cookies smell so good, he knew. Might it not do the same for the soap?

Carefully Will placed the bottle on the wide shelf that held the bread box and flour bin, and jumped down. In a few minutes he had poured the entire contents of the bottle into the soap frame. He watched with satisfaction as the vanilla made pretty brown streaks all over the still warm soap, then slowly disappeared from view.

Later that day, Manda set about to make a cake for supper.

"Polly, where is the vanilla?"

Polly looked up from the bread she was kneading. "On the second shelf."

"No, it isn't."

"I put it there myself when I finished baking yesterday. Almost full, it was. It didn't walk off by itself." She hurried over to the cupboard. "Well, I'll be. It ain't there, is it! Guess you'll have to use the lemon extract until we find it."

Before darkness fell, Luke brought the soap bars indoors in a burlap bag and set them down by the stove.

"There you are, ladies. They'll harden up more, but they're cut and ready."

Polly took out a bar and turned it over in her hand. Then she put it to her nose.

"I found the vanilla," she announced. "And I think I know how it got there. I just hope I'm around the day that child tries to eat one of these."

THE NEW HOUSE

About the middle of July, Chad announced that he would be going to town again to pick up supplies. Both Manda and Polly sat down that very afternoon with pen and paper.

"The first thing on here is going to be oilcloth," said Polly. "I'm tired of trying to wash dust off these rough wooden shelves. This table could use a little color too. The brightest you can find."

"We're going to need lightweight goods for shirts and dresses," Manda reminded her. "As hot as it is now, Chad says the real summer heat hasn't even started."

As Polly checked the cupboards and continued her list, Manda wrote a letter to her friend Lydia.

We have been in South Dakota for two months now, and it would not be possible to describe to you all that is here and all that has happened. I will do the best I can.

The soddy in which we live is spacious enough, since almost everything save sleeping is done outside. Chad built bunk beds for Frances and Alice and the two younger boys. This conserves much space. Ethan sleeps in the bunkhouse with the men.

I thank the Lord that it is cool inside, for the sun is relentless, and one's strength is gone before midday. The children are as brown as the Indians, and growing at an astonishing speed. Simon turned five before we left, you know, and Will was four in June. Alice will be seven this month. Ethan will not be ten until November, but already he works alongside the men.

The Indians who helped with the soddy are going to work with Chad on the house. They are friendly people and have been a great help to us. Silver Wing even showed me how to make ink! When the men sharpened the tools, we gathered the filings made and dissolved them in vinegar. Maple bark was boiled and added to provide tannic acid. It gives the ink its color as well as makes it last longer, Silver Wing told us. The Indians are remarkably wise in the ways of nature.

Frances takes great comfort in her organ. I'm glad we prevailed upon Chad to bring it. We have found that Simon is uncommonly talented in music. He can not only sing any tune he hears, but is able to pick it out on the organ. All the children have learned hymns, and as a congregation of ten on Sunday mornings, we do quite well. Lessons will not begin until winter forces us to spend more time inside.

I miss my comfortable home, but I must admit that there is something about the prairie that draws one. The sky looks like a bowl turned over the earth, and there is nothing between us and *sunsets. Even Polly stops her chores to look at the wonder of God's handiwork. Luke has studied the heavens and pointed out the constellations to the children. The nights are so clear that the stars seem ready to drop on us. Indeed we see them shooting across the skies nightly, much to the delight of us all.*

I will be glad when cooler weather comes. I don't tolerate the heat as well as the others do. Polly has her usual boundless energy, and the children are thriving.

Chad and Henry will go to town tomorrow, and our letters will be posted. Please write when you can. This is lonely country.

As ever,
Manda

"We have our lists of errands ready for you," Manda told Chad at supper time.

"Errands? We aren't going to have time for errands. I have business at the bank and land office, and Henry is going to pick up some pigs and feed and paint for the house. The new roofing should be here, and the windows will be ready. We're not going to have any extra time."

"You have a family to provide for too," Manda reminded him. "But you can take us all with you, if you'd like."

Chad looked up from his plate in alarm.

Frances recognized her opportunity. "I'll go, Papa. I can shop for the dress goods and things like that."

Chad was relieved. "Yes, I guess you can. But we won't have time for any playing around. It will be a busy day."

Manda didn't continue the conversation, and everyone

present knew why. Chad's mention of paint for the house reminded them all that Manda was still less than enthusiastic about their soon-to-be house on the prairie.

Shortly after they'd arrived at the homestead, Chad had ridden over to the Indian reservation to arrange for the men to return to work. They came early the next morning to begin digging the foundation. Manda had already approved the spot that was chosen on which to build the house.

"There's a good bit of shade along that row of cottonwood trees," she said to Polly. "We can have a spring house right at the corner near the kitchen."

"What kind of house is that?" Alice asked.

"You know where the spring is that keeps our milk and meat cold? The men will build a little house around it that it can be used as a cooler for the food. That's where our drinking water comes from too."

It seemed that all but the littlest children had ideas for the new house.

"I want my kitchen facing the east," Polly said. "It's more cheerful in the morning, and the hot afternoon sun isn't beating through the windows when I'm getting supper."

"I'll need a parlor, Papa," Frances said. "You can't put an organ in just any room. Besides, we need a nice place to entertain visitors."

"There ain't no one within entertaining distance of this place," Polly told her. "But having a few extra rooms so people can spread out and get out from under my feet won't be a bad idea."

Henry and Luke thought that the bunkhouse where they now slept would do nicely for them. "A little more padding to keep the cold out come winter is all we'll need. It's up to Ethan whether he wants to stay or not."

"I do," Ethan said. "I like my corner."

"I want to stay out there too!" Simon decided.

"Will is going to need someone to share his room," Manda said. "He's not used to being alone at night. You're the next biggest boy we have to take care of him."

"I guess I'll have to stay in the house, then. Will you mind, Ethan?"

Ethan assured him that he wouldn't. "It's not like we'll be living in different places. I'll just be sleeping out there."

"Seems to me like Chad is mighty agreeable to everything we ask for," Polly remarked when she and Manda were working alone in the soddy. "That ain't like him."

Manda nodded. "The same thought came to me. But for the life of me I don't know what he's up to. It's as if he doesn't want to get into a discussion about the house for fear we'll find out something he's keeping from us."

The two women went to work in the garden, and for a few moments they watched the men pouring the foundation. Ethan carried water to mix with the sand and gravel for cement. Men with hoes spread the mixture evenly over the area that had been laid out for a concrete slab. There seemed to be nothing out of line, and Manda shook her head as she bent to her weeding. She was being too suspicious, she thought.

Finally the foundation was finished, and the Indians didn't appear in the morning to work. By the time Manda noticed that there was no activity around the place, Chad had disappeared to the four corners of the property.

Polly had another observation. "Nothin' out there to work with. How come we ain't seen no lumber to start the frame?"

Manda lost no time in approaching Chad on that subject when he returned for supper.

"Chad, when is the lumber being delivered for the house? They've finished the cement work. You've ordered it, haven't you?"

Chad didn't look up from his plate. "That foundation needs time to dry and cure before a house is put on it. We don't want cracks in there before we've gone through one winter. Everything will be done in good time."

With that Manda had to be content. However, when another week went by with no apparent progress, she became annoyed.

"What in the world is holding them up? At this rate we won't be out of this soddy until next summer."

"Can't be the cement," Polly said. "The sun's so hot it's already baked the dirt. The foundation has to be set."

So once again, Manda questioned Chad.

"Did something happen that you can't get the lumber? How long ago did you order it?"

Chad cleared his throat and looked uncomfortable.

"Well, actually, I haven't."

"Chad! Why ever not? You know how long it takes anything to get out here by train! What are you waiting for?"

"I guess you might as well know, Manda. I don't intend to order any lumber." He stopped and pulled his handkerchief out and mopped his face. "We . . . uh . . . we already have a house."

Manda turned pale and stared at Chad in alarm.

"Have you been in the sun too long? There's no house out there!"

"I've heard of them there merges," Polly muttered.

"Mirages," Manda said, and then the terrible thought occurred to her. "Chad, have you decided to let us continue to live in this soddy?"

"No, of course not," Chad replied. "I told you—we have a house."

"And just when might we be able to see it?"

"Now Manda, don't lose your temper. Just let me explain. There was a family homesteading a mile or so up river, and they decided to give up and go back south."

"I can't imagine why," Manda snapped.

"I can," Polly put in.

"Do you want to hear this or not? They built a good house on the place, and we can have it for moving it off the land."

Manda leaned back in her chair. "Moving it. You're going to take it apart and bring the lumber down here and put it up again?"

"Don't have to do that. We'll move the house just as it

stands and put it on our own foundation. The Indians will jack up the corners and put logs under them, then use their oxen to pull it down here. You don't know how fortunate we were to get this place."

"No, I guess I don't. Instead of living in my own home, I'll have a secondhand house."

"You haven't even seen it yet. You'll be pleased. We'll put on a new roof, and it will need new windows. You can have whatever color paint you want."

Manda said no more, but went to her sewing machine and began treading furiously as she ran up the seams on the sheets she had turned. Chad seemed to be searching for something more to say, but finally he turned and left.

Polly splashed water into the dishpan and banged the pots and pans on the table.

"When I was about six years old," she said, "Ma took apart Pa's old overcoat and cut one out for me. She told me I could have any buttons on it that I could find in her basket. That was supposed to make it just like new." Polly paused with her hands in soapy water. "Come to think of it, that coat did keep me warm for a couple of winters. I reckon that house will shelter us, even if it ain't your first choice."

Manda had to agree, but she was disappointed. "I'll have to admit that we may be able to get into it sooner. It just wasn't what I had in mind."

Now Chad, Henry, and Frances were in the wagon, ready to leave for town. The day promised to be hot again, and they wanted to be on the way before the sun was any higher. Manda turned her attention to Frances.

"Are you sure that the list is in your reticule? Do you have your parasol? Just because you live out here on the plains doesn't mean you can't have a good complexion. Stay out of the sun as much as possible."

Frances tied her broad-brimmed hat under her chin. "Yes, Mama."

"And keep your gloves on. You don't need to look as though you worked in the fields."

"Yes, Mama."

Manda turned to Chad. "Please don't forget to pick up our mail. And remember the upholstery tacks at the hardware. Will you be home by dark?"

"Not if we don't get started. Don't fuss, Manda. We all know how to take care of ourselves, and we're not likely to forget anything. You sure you don't want to go along?"

Manda stepped back from the wagon and shook her head. "No, thank you. I'll make the trip when the weather is cooler."

The wagon rattled along the dry, rutted trail, and the three passengers rode in silence for some time. Frances was busy with her visions of freedom. With luck, she thought, she could finish her shopping before the others did and have time to sit in the hotel lobby. She remembered with pleasure their arrival in Winner and the opportunity she'd had to observe the comings and goings of people who traveled through.

Chad and Henry were busy with their own thoughts.

Chad felt that he had struck a good bargain on the house. Many buildings, he was told, were moved from one homestead to another when their owners gave up the fight to tame the prairie. "Give up" was not a phrase in Chad's vocabulary. He hadn't become successful by abandoning a project when it became too difficult. He was prepared to claim his land whatever obstacles appeared in his path. When the house was in place and Manda was able to direct the painting and papering, she would be satisfied. He should have told her of his plans sooner, but discussing his business, even with his wife, was still difficult for Chad.

Henry looked across the open space and was thankful to be living and breathing on this hot July day. His close brush with death had given him a new appreciation for all he had. The work was hard, but part of his reward would be in land in this new territory. Someday, perhaps, he would have his own home and family. The wagon was not yet out of sight of the acres that he and Luke had planted. The wheat was growing well. The words of a song that had been popular for about five years came to Henry, and he sang them over to himself.

"O beautiful for spacious skies,
For amber waves of grain . . . ."

Surely the author must have been writing about South Dakota.

Chad's voice broke into his thoughts. "We're going to need rain right soon. The prairie grass is so dry that there's danger of fire. Sun is good for the wheat, though. We're going to miss our threshing machine and baler this fall."

Henry squinted at the sky. "Doesn't look much like rain today. It could hold until we get our supplies back home, far as I'm concerned."

"Papa, does the house have two floors?"

"Yes, four rooms upstairs and four rooms down. I think we'll build a summer kitchen so that Polly will have a place to do her canning and baking."

"What color will the house be?"

"Your mother favors white with a green trim. The roofing is green."

"Mama wishes she had brought some roses or a lilac bush. Would they grow out here?"

"I'm sure they would," Chad replied. "We'll try to find something to surprise her."

"I think she'll like it better than the last surprise you gave her," Frances said. "I can hardly wait to see that house move across the prairie."

"There's something else moving across the prairie right now. Look." Henry pointed ahead of them. "Antelope. And they're really traveling."

They watched the herd for as long as they could see it. It was the most exciting thing they'd encountered on the trail all morning, and Frances was glad to see signs of life as they approached the town of Winner. She had plans for her day.

SETTLED IN

Chad brought the wagon to a stop in front of the blacksmith shop, and Frances looked around her with pleasure. Winner was a prairie town with very little to recommend it to the world. The main street was rutted and dusty, and the trails leading into it were nothing more than one-way wagon tracks. Its only claim to the title "town" was a railway station. There were three sets of tracks; two accommodated the twice-daily north- and southbound trains, and the third was siding that went nowhere.

Winner served a purpose, however. Located just one and a half counties east of the Missouri River on the isolated plains, it was the stopping-off place for goods ordered from mail-order houses and manufacturers in the east. It drew homesteaders from all around the territory to pick up equipment necessary for establishing their portion of the great state of South Dakota.

All of this meant little to Frances as she anticipated the day ahead of her. She had frequently shopped with her mother, but never alone. The list and the money in her handbag gave her a feeling of independence. After retying her hat ribbons and smoothing her gloves, she allowed herself to be helped from the wagon.

"Do you have your mother's and Polly's mail to post?"

"Yes, Papa."

"You're sure you can manage the shopping by yourself?"

"Yes, Papa."

"You know where the hotel is. We'll meet you there for dinner at one o'clock."

"Yes, Papa." Frances was impatient to get started on her adventure.

Finally Chad strode across the street to the bank, and Henry disappeared into the hardware store. Frances picked her way slowly down the boardwalk fronted by the Mercantile, Jay's Saloon, the Star Restaurant, and Maude's Millinery. At the end of the block stood the Winner Hotel, where the family had stayed when they first arrived.

The Mercantile, where Frances would be shopping, would be the last stop. First she must look in every window on the street, except, of course, the saloon. For the first time in her life there was no one to hurry her along, and Frances meant to take advantage of it.

One window of the restaurant revealed tables set and a few customers lingering over their coffee. The other window contained all manner of baked goods. Rolls, bread, cakes, and pies were displayed in tempting array. A large cake declared "Happy Birthday, Sophia." A menu and price list on the window said that one could have ham, eggs, fried potatoes, and griddle cakes for 25¢.

She continued on toward the milliner's. Hats of every description were arrayed before her. Frances took in every detail from the simple wide-brimmed straw variety, like the one she was wearing, to ornate head coverings with every form of trimming imaginable. Oh, to be a grown lady with places to go that would require a hat like one of these!

For a moment Frances forgot that her station in life was more suited to a calico sunbonnet, which she would purchase at the Mercantile. She pictured herself in the gorgeous green velvet with an attractive feather falling gracefully over her face. After considering each hat in turn, and noting that most of them sold for at least $2.75, Frances finally turned away from the window with a sigh and directed her attention to the Mercantile.

This was the store where one could obtain anything necessary for running a home and family. Choices were limited only by the amount of money one had to spend. Frances was aware that Mama had calculated the cost of her goods on her list to the last penny, but it certainly wouldn't hurt to look around and imagine that she might purchase one of everything she fancied.

Oilcloth	3 yds	@5¢	$0.15
Sunbonnet			
Large	3	@22¢	$0.66
Small	1	@12¢	$0.12

Dress goods	24 yds	@10¢	$2.40
	18 yds	@8 1/2¢	$1.53
Lace	10 yds	@2 1/2¢	$0.25
Thread	4	@3¢	$0.12

Mama had sent $6.00 with the list, and she would be sure to expect the 77¢ change to be returned to her. Frances could hear her say, "Papa doesn't prosper by having us waste his money."

She made her purchases, dropped the change into her bag, and carried the package to the wagon. A trip to the post office, and she would be free to go to the hotel. The wagon already had a number of things in it that the men had bought and covered with a tarp, so Frances pushed her packages under the seat and crossed the street. She passed the bank and the land office and was about to enter the post office when she stopped in her tracks before a sign on the building:

Dr. Robert James, M.D.
Dr. Timothy Flynn, M.D.
Office Upstairs

The young man from the train! Did she dare go upstairs and greet him? What would Papa say? Frances stood considering the impossible. She knew what Papa would say. A young lady would not be so bold as to be the first to speak to a gentleman. Reluctantly she walked on. It was nearing time to meet Henry and Papa for dinner, and she wouldn't have very long to sit in the lobby and watch the people.

Among the letters from home was one from her friend Rebecca, and Frances hurried to the hotel to read it. So interested was she in the news it contained she didn't notice how dark the sky had become. A sudden flash of lightning and a crash of thunder caused her to drop the letter and jump to her feet in alarm.

"Allow me," a voice said, then, "How do you do, Miss Rush?"

Frances stared at the young man who had stooped beside her to retrieve the letter.

"The thunder startled me," Frances said. "I wasn't expecting to see you. We didn't know you were a doctor." Her face turned red as she realized that she was babbling.

The young man appeared not to notice. "I guess I didn't mention it. I came to Winner because my future wife lives here, and I was invited to go into practice with her father. Elaine and I will be married in August." He looked around the lobby. "Have you come with your family?"

"Just my father and Henry. Here they come now."

The young man was introduced to Chad and Henry and invited to have dinner with them.

"I'm truly sorry that I must decline," he said, "but I have office hours in just a few minutes. Will you be staying in town overnight?"

"No, we'll leave as soon as the rain lets up. Perhaps next time we are in town." They shook hands, and Dr. Flynn went out into the wet afternoon.

Frances watched him leave. She might have known that

a young man like that would be spoken for. Oh, well. He was probably ten years older than she anyway. She was dreaming to think that he would pay special attention to her.

"Frances? We're going in to dinner. Are you going to stand there until we get back?"

Frances sighed and followed her father and Henry to the dining room.

The storm passed as quickly as it had come, and by the time they had finished eating, they were able to start for home.

"The rain is headed west," Henry remarked. "We're following right along behind it."

"We can use it," Chad said. "It certainly has settled the dust on this road."

"It didn't make it any cooler," Frances said. "I feel like I'm steaming."

"It will start to cool soon," Chad replied. "We'll be home before dark, the Lord willing."

When the wagon had headed for town in the early morning light, the remaining members of the household gathered for breakfast around the outdoor table.

"This is going to be one hot day," Luke said. "I don't like the feel of it."

"What does it feel like, Luke?" Simon asked.

"Don't know. Something's coming though."

Everyone looked at the sky.

"There isn't a cloud in sight," Manda said. "When the sun comes up it will be just like yesterday—unbearable."

"The air is heavy," Luke insisted. He nodded toward the wash tub on the open fire. "You picked the wrong time to do clothes."

"I don't 'pick' a time to wash," Polly snapped. "When no one has anything clean to wear, the day is here. And with ten people mucking around in this dirt, that's most every day." She stomped off to stir the clothes in the boiling water.

Luke chuckled. "Weather don't help her disposition none either."

As the morning wore on, the heat became more intense and the air more oppressive. Manda found it difficult to stay with her sewing, and she made frequent trips to the door of the soddy to study the sky. The younger children played listlessly beside the river, and Polly muttered under her breath as she pounded the bread dough. Manda wished that Chad hadn't chosen this day to go to town. Even if he were working out of sight in the field, she would feel better.

When Simon came running across the yard, shouting for her to come and see, Manda rushed to the door.

"Look! Look what's coming!" He pointed toward the north.

There in the distance was a large object moving across the prairie so slowly that Manda wasn't certain that it was moving at all. She knew at once what it was.

"It's that wretched house," she said to Polly, who had come to stand beside her. "That must have been what Luke felt was coming."

Polly wiped her hands on her apron. " 'Tain't natural,

moving houses across the country like that. A house is supposed to stand where you build it, not go chasing from one place to another. How long you reckon it will take to get here?"

When Luke and Ethan came in for dinner, the object appeared to be no nearer than it had been when Simon spotted it.

"It will take several days," Luke said. "They have to rest the oxen and change teams pretty often. That's a heavy load to drag without wheels under it."

By the middle of the afternoon the house wasn't the only thing coming across the prairie. In the northeast sky, black clouds began rolling toward them. Lightning flashed and thunder rumbled and growled in the distance. Polly herded the children into the soddy, and they huddled in the doorway, watching the approaching storm. The chickens and ducks scattered, and Ethan led the cows to the barn. Suddenly the sky opened up, and hailstones of enormous size began to beat the ground.

"Big snow!" Will shouted, and he had to be restrained from running out to grab some of them.

"You stay here," Polly told him. "These things would knock you senseless. How in the world ice can drop from the sky on a day as hot as this, I'll never know."

When the storm moved on, the ground was covered with a blanket of white, much to the joy of the children. Luke, however, did not share their excitement. He gazed out over the flattened fields where corn and grain had been standing proudly that morning. His shoulders drooped, and his usually cheerful face was glum.

"Seems like if the Lord told you to pick up and move to this forsaken plain, He'd at least see to it that your crops didn't get beat to the ground the first summer you was here."

Manda was silent, for she felt much the same way herself. They had suffered a great deal for a lot of nothing. Ethan stood beside them with his fists stuffed into his overall pockets.

"What will Chad do when he sees it?"

"I can tell you what he'll do," Polly said. "He'll save what he can, plow the rest under, and plant again. Mebbe I shouldn't bring it up, but the Bible says that the Lord sends rain on the just and on the unjust. Same thing for ice balls, I guess. The unjust will complain about it, and the just will make the best of it. Seems to me like I read that the just shall live by faith, so we got to buck up and believe that we'll be taken care of. Now I'm goin' to get supper and be thankful for what we got."

If Chad was discouraged by the apparent futility of his hard work, he didn't reveal it to the family. As Polly had predicted, he continued to labor in the fields and do what he could to restore the crops.

"We'll have late wheat and corn," he said, "and there will be wild hay for the stock." He looked at Manda. "You were right to bring all our winter food. We'll not go hungry, and we will have adequate shelter. We must thank the Lord for keeping us well and providing for our needs."

The "adequate shelter" was approaching its intended spot, however slowly. It was now possible to determine the outlines of the house, and by the end of the week, the children were counting the windows on the sides visible to them.

"There are two windows in every bedroom." Frances announced. "I hope mine looks out over the river."

"I won't fuss about my bedroom as long as my kitchen looks east," Polly said. "What will they do if they are hauling that thing up here backwards?"

"By the looks of the size of it, we'll just have to live in it backwards," Manda said.

"Don't worry about that," Chad replied when she asked him about it. "Comancho knows how we want it. As a matter of fact, that's the way it sat on the original lot."

"How convenient. I don't suppose the cupboards are in place and the floors scrubbed?"

"No, but if we had started building from the ground up, we'd be spending the winter in the soddy. I'm sure you'll be more comfortable in the house, even if it isn't exactly what you had planned."

"Yes, I know I will," Manda admitted. "I have no cause to complain. The Lord has been good to us. When I see the size of the rooms, I'll order wallpaper, and we'll begin sewing on the curtains."

The day the house was lowered to the foundation was an exciting one for everybody. Aside from feeding and milking, farm work was suspended. There was much shouting of directions and scurrying about by Comancho and his helpers. Even Polly left her housework to watch this unusual event. She was alarmed by the sight of men crawling underneath the house before the logs were removed.

"I hope they don't let that down on nobody. What if the house don't fit on that piece of cement?"

"They're putting big blocks of brick between the cement slab and the house. And it will fit. You wait and see," Henry told her.

Polly didn't argue, but she looked skeptical. However, by the middle of the afternoon the logs were pulled out, and the house settled solidly on its foundation.

"Can we move in now?" Simon shouted.

"Not yet," Frances told him. "It needs a new roof, and fixing up inside. It will take awhile to do all that."

As Ethan walked from the barn with Henry, he looked at the big house and the surrounding fields.

"I guess we really belong here now, don't we?" he said.

Henry put his arm around the boy.

"You certainly do, Ethan. We couldn't get along without any one of you. Come on—let's see what Polly has fixed for supper. And afterward I'll beat you in a game of checkers."

The Orphans' Journey

Book One—
Looking for Home

Eight years old, and Ethan is in charge.

With their mama dead and their pa gone, there is no way the nine Cooper children can stay together. The four young ones must go to an orphanage.

Ethan, Alice, Simon, and Will settle in at the Briarlane Christian Children's Home where there's plenty to eat, plenty of work, and, it seems to Ethan, plenty of talk about a God who cares about every detail of their lives.

In spite of his own worries, Ethan takes seriously his charge to look after his sister and brothers. Whether the threat comes from a bullying older boy, a disgruntled hog, or a wealthy lady, Ethan is ready to do battle to protect his family. But maybe he could use some extra help . . . like the care of the "Good Shepherd" the folks at Briarlane seem to know.

Arleta Richardson is the author of the beloved Grandma's Attic series as well as the Orphans' Journey series.

Chariot Books™

The Orphans' Journey

Book Two—
Whistle-stop West

"Are you sure they know there's four of us?"

Ethan can't believe that one couple will adopt all
four of the Cooper children—Ethan, Alice, Simon, and
Will—but Mr. and Mrs. Rush are ready to welcome
them to their farm in Nebraska. So the Coopers board
the Orphan Train—along with twenty-one other
orphans looking for a new home—and head west.

They find plenty of adventure along the way as
railroad cars seem to appear and disappear, and they
encounter their first prairie dust storm. And with
each stop the Orphan Train makes, more of their
friends find new homes.

Though Ethan still isn't sure about what will be
waiting for them at the end of the line, he does know
that "there is one Friend who will be with them, no
matter where they go."

Arleta Richardson is the author of the beloved
Grandma's Attic series as well as the Orphans'
Journey series.

Chariot Books™

Are you looking for fun ways to bring the Bible to life in the lives of your children?

Chariot Family Publishing has hundreds of books, toys, games, and videos that help teach your children the Bible and apply it to their everyday lives.

Look for these educational, inspirational, and fun products at your local Christian bookstore.